DREAMING OF A HOPEFUL DEATH

A. S. MORI

Dreaming of a Hopeful Death

A. S. Mori

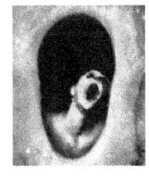

CONTENTS

PREFACE

Dear beloved reader,

Though I believe this book needs no preface, I feel that since this is one of the few opportunities for me to speak directly to the reader, I intend to take full advantage of it without overstaying my welcome.

Dreaming of a Hopeful Death is an introspective and philosophical sci-fi journey through the universe which tries to answer the question of what would happen if the entirety of the human race had its free will taken away and was forced on an unending trip through space until the heat death of the universe. I am of the opinion that the themes of mortality, legacy, nihilism and time are universally shared and that existentialist questions can best be accessibly presented in the form of a narrative which is why this novel exists and why I put in the hard work required to bring it to fruition.

With regards to the heat death theory of the universe, many elements were drawn from prevailing theories in cosmology. With that said, certain details may become out of date in the near future due to discoveries made by space telescopes like the JWST (James Webb Space Telescope). Regardless of how the science changes in the future, I believe that the main themes that drive the novel will be eternally relevant.

It should be noted that this is a book with one character which represents the entirety of the human race. This character is composed of many different personalities and parts. As a result, this character uses the pronouns "I" and "we" interchangeably. Do not be confused when this occurs. Regardless of the pronoun, the main character is still the same and remains the same throughout the novel whenever first person pronouns are used (with the exception of the prologue, the first chapters of each of the four main parts, and the epilogue which utilize a narrator).

Additionally, there are many aspects of this book that are open ended. There are many questions that are asked and in many cases, very few answers that are provided. The reason for this is because I would prefer that each reader comes to their own interpretation of the questions and if possible their own answers. This is an exploration of ideas first and foremost.

Finally, I want to thank you for beginning this novel and hope you discover something about yourself and your existence along the way.

Sincerely,

A.S. Mori

PROLOGUE

Once upon a time, there was a witch who lived within a forest deep within the territory of a burgeoning kingdom that was in the midst of turmoil. This witch was a master of magic, potions and alchemy whose practice has continued for centuries since she first resolved to become proficient in the occult arts in an era long forgotten by history. With ambition and persistence, she brought herself from the level of a newcomer to that of a virtuoso within her areas of expertise.

Her livelihood was typically one of a relaxed solitude and hermitage. The domain of man seldom reached her doorstep until recently as a result of the fierce beasts that prowled the forest floors and the vegetation that spanned the savage reaches of nature's dominion resulting in a labyrinth of hostile paths that were punctuated by oases of abundance and bucolic bliss. It was in one such oasis that this witch resided. In the past, the witch lived in peace and practiced her spells in isolation as her predecessors, the teachers who nurtured her when she was young centuries ago, once did. It was through her skills as a user of magic that she tamed the forest and kept it at bay to allow for her life of relative luxury.

Occasionally, a traveler wandered into her oasis; sometimes by accident, sometimes intentionally. Initially, the witch acted cordially, healing the wounds of travelers and teaching them of the ways of the forest. With time, as those from the civilized world began to grow less fearful of the forest, the lost traveler was replaced by the prospecting adventurer who wished for profit within the impenetrable woods. This led to unpleasant encounters where strangers intruded into her home in search of elixirs of immortality, gold, and knowledge. A decision needed to be made on the proper course of action and this decision resulted in a large-scale circle of transmutation which surrounded the witch's territory. Much like hellebore used by farmers to conveniently keep annoying pests at bay, a simple action by the witch spelled doom for interlopers. All who failed to heed the warnings placed on the edges of the circle were cursed to rapidly turn to stone when they trespassed into the domain of the witch. Those who entered were turned to stone, and those who witnessed this phenomenon reported back to those in the nearby kingdom which was nearing the end of its rule. The king sentenced the witch to be burnt at the stake. However, regardless of how many enforcers attempted to execute their justice, all were turned to stone. These invaders who met the same fate were petrified into magnificent figures that appeared as though they were seemingly sculpted out of marble, granite, and sometimes jade and added to the makeshift gallery that surrounded the area. Despite the cruel nature of the punishment, it was a stunning sight to see armies of people from all walks of life collected in one place. This by itself acted as a draw for some foolhardy admirers like fish to lures, and the collection only grew.

Eventually, these excursions into the forest by these invaders declined as the kingdom reached the end of its tenure. The statues withered to dust, and the kingdom which encroached upon the edge of the forest retreated as an extended civil war split the kingdom into two factions. One kingdom became two, and centuries passed until former conflicts were revived to result in the new kingdom neighboring the forest gradually being conquered by its enemy piece by piece. The royal family was being hunted and escaped by foot into the forest. The king, queen, princess, and their retainers wandered the labyrinth of vines and pines only to become more and more entwined in its disorienting layout. The king fell ill, and the queen starved, both passing together in the night. The malnourished retainers who were left were eaten by wolves leaving the princess to wander aimlessly in the woods and fend for herself against the treacherous surroundings.

Crawling through the thickets, her hands bled as she blindly scrambled in the dark in search of shelter. Sharp jabs of pain could be felt running across her body in an agonizing mix of fatigue and injury. After hours of searching, her hopes were met in the form of a clearing partially illuminated by the moonlight. Shadows splayed along the grass floor as she stepped into the clearing with a sense of relief. Upon approaching the shadows, it became clear they held a humanoid form. A rigidness set upon her feet as she looked down to see an unyielding petrification feed on her body from the ground up. She craned her head to peer at the others and realized they were those who were met with the fate she was to suffer. She reached out with a hand, as though to ask for help, and it was in that position she stayed as stone crawled upon her arm to leave her as a landmark. Unable to speak, unable to move, unable to ask for help. Perhaps it was mercy, perhaps it was an oversight, but she was left with her senses. It was then that the princess was met with a realization: those who came before her may be in the same predicament.

Doomed to live, but deprived of life.

She wished to call out, for someone to help. She wished that someone could save her. Unfortunately, the witch no longer resided in the forest. Her absence marked the end of a dynasty. Either due to disappointment, disdain, or a simple wish to move on, the witch departed from the realm of men in search of that which could satisfy her desires. The only thing she left behind were the statues that she effortlessly made without much thought anymore. Whether she would return was unknown.

PART 1
Wishes from a Past Far Gone

CHAPTER 1: THE CURSE

It is not always evolutionarily advantageous to be able to comprehend the fragility of one's life and one's race. In the past, whether a meteor was about to impact the earth, or a galaxy could collide with the Milky Way was of no concern to the common man. Humanity's concerns were not only terrestrial, but primarily individual even when considering social contexts. This was true not only of Homo sapiens, but their predecessors as well despite such cosmic events being existential in nature.

We do not perceive everything, and our senses are fundamentally flawed when considering what lies beyond our senses and our intellectual abilities to comprehend what is not. The sensory organs are limited to certain aspects of reality, and it is the responsibility of the brain to properly interpret the data provided by these organs. For example, sight is not images captured by the eyes, but rather images constructed using data captured by the eyes based on the light it is able to perceive. Both of these components are inherently flawed, and as a result, the images that are sensed are not a perfect representation of reality.

To supplement our shortcomings, we use tools such as eyeglasses, telescopes, microscopes, as well as sensors that convert from other spectra and streams into a format we understand. These too have a limitation in that they are the creations of humans. These humans are subject to human error, to misconceptions, and to a simple limitation of intellect and body. There could easily be forms of energy, matter, and states of being beyond their capabilities that, to them, may as well not exist as there is no way to sense or observe them. They believe that mathematics can overcome such shortcomings as it is pure information and logic. However, whether the mathematics developed by human civilization has a complete foundation is also questionable. Like basic arithmetic and the concept of zero, there may be holes in the understanding of modern mathematics and its foundation which conceals entire branches of the field to the most talented of its practitioners. Even here, when humanity tries to free itself of reality and operate upon pure information, there are obstacles.

Furthermore, reality holds an abundance of information that must be parsed to be made sense of. Not all information is useful, and as a result, living organisms typically take advantage of that which is beneficial to the prolonging of its life and species and what it is even capable of processing. Humanity is no exception. There is much which is not perceived, and much which is not known. From the smallest building block of reality to the entirety of the unobservable universe, although there is much to learn of within a single lifetime, there is infinitely more that will never be known even when given the lifetime of the universe to explore it.

Despite this, human civilization has advanced its desire for knowledge in its eternal mission to minimize its pain, maximize its pleasure, and master its manipulation of the reality in which it is confined in. In doing so, it advanced, while inflicting itself with artificial sufferings, to its pinnacle. With a neo-liberalist global economy that valued continuous growth above all else, it advanced, day by day, quarter by quarter. The system was effective due to its iterative nature, but ill-suited for thinking beyond the short term which meant that it was suboptimal. It was suboptimal to the point that there were rudimentary algorithms capable of better planning in the short term as well as the long term. It was not that humans were less intelligent. It was rather that human nature was superseded efficiency and outcomes. This suboptimal nature was not recognized as a problem to be solved because there were many who benefited directly from it despite humanity as a whole being unable to reach its full potential as a result. It was very rarely that cosmic timescales were even considered or even long term timescales that were relevant within a lifetime. This is partially what led to the downfall of the modern human race, but even if human civilization managed to recognize its lack of knowledge as a severe existential threat, with its level of technology and confinement to the third dimension, it would have still been powerless to escape its fate. No amount of vision could overcome a lack of drive and concern to prevent all horrors that could possibly be out there.

Ignorant of the large-scale phenomena that occur in other dimensions, humanity was unaware of the occurrences and beings that resided within higher dimensions and was naturally unprepared for the fate they would be cursed to for the remainder of all time. Like stepping on an ant is to a human, an eldritch being operating beyond the third dimension mutated all living humans into a single entity within an instant. Unlike a naturally occurring process that had a beginning and an end, the transformation was immediate and ignored traditional understandings of cause and effect. In one moment, humanity was composed of multiple individuals going about their daily lives. In the next, humanity was one entity with the memories of all living humans at the time, leaving the earth to all other species to fill the void. Society and civilization became one sentient being and in doing so, the nature of human existence was forever changed.

To describe the god that lived beyond the third dimension is a fool's errand. To explain the purpose of its action is equally pointless. A being that is not visible within our reality, which does not hold the same emotional motivations and most probably acts upon a set of morals that transcends traditional conceptions of right and wrong that holds meaning to those like us is beyond words. Time for such a being is not an arrow that moves in one direction, but rather a plane that allows for travel through time, space, and through an infinite number of possibilities. In fact, even that description may be subpar as time may be more of a hyperplane. It is likely that such a being was not only able to travel through multiple realities, but also multiple universes which each held their own rules by which they operated. With that said, stories of other universes are beyond the scope of humanity's new state of being. In other parallel realities, perhaps humanity was spared. However, in this one, this specific one, humanity was forced into singularity and eternal life. Its existence was now that of a singular entity unable to die or physically interact with the physical world until the universe reaches heat death. Its role in the universe was no longer that of an active player, but rather an observer unable to act upon reality or conversely be acted upon. Its future was now one that was sentenced to wander the universe like a sorrowful ghost that haunted the empty spaces between solar systems and planets—a Sisyphus of the cosmos.

CHAPTER 2: BIRTH

Prior to opening my eyes, I had what I thought was a dream. I dreamed a dream, but I don't sleep anymore. So, that cannot be what it was. Maybe it was a vision. Maybe it was a trance or a hallucination instead. I was standing, unclothed in a grassy plain on a clear, sunny day. I have no recollection of how I arrived there, but I was there, and I was calm, as though I belonged there. The endless ripples of green which undulated up to the horizon were punctuated by clusters of trees and ended in a mountain range that rose up in the distance to meet cumulus clouds that filled the deep blue above with small puffs of white and gray. The grass beneath my feet felt young and fertile. There was not a hint of death in the surroundings, only emptiness. Not a plant that lacked vibrancy, and no sign of aging anywhere to be seen. It was lush, it was pristine, and it was lonely: an Eden for one.

I peered around to glimpse an androgynous humanoid figure in the distance atop a hill. Perhaps the figure saw me as well since it craned its neck, towards me. I ruminated on whether I should approach it for what felt like minutes, before taking my first step in the direction of the only other person I could see in this vacant land. With each step, I breathed the fresh air in, and gained more clarity on what was in the distance. The figure did the same, approaching me gradually, languidly swinging its arms in the same manner as me as it navigated the decline down from the hill as I climbed my way up. With the sun to its back, I had trouble making out its features. It was as though it was a standing shadow, a featureless humanoid that was only capable of action. I saw it place its arms to its mouth. I think it was trying to speak, but I heard nothing. As I got closer, I could make out the details, fingers, ears, and a nose. I tried to call back, in an attempt to communicate, but I could not. I too was the same.

We advanced. I was within speaking distance, ready for conversation, but I could not utter a word. I could try making signs with my hands, but I did not know if it would understand. The lighting did not help, so I stepped around the figure, placing the sun to my back. The figure's head followed me, and I could finally discern the details. I could see the eyes, the color of its pupils, and the uncertainty in its gaze. I could see the texture of its skin and the pores on its face, each strand of hair, each eyelash, and each vein. There was a sense of hope on its face, as though we could reach a state of unity, friendship, or something more. It was a deep longing that stemmed from a deeply embedded primal instinct. Then its eyes glanced behind me, and I saw a shadow cover the sun in its eyes and the face turn to one of apprehension. I turned around to see another figure. It was one with the same face, same hands, and same body— a clone of sorts. I heard muffled footsteps and glanced in the direction of the sound to see another, and another, and another. With each individual that made an appearance, was an individual with an identical appearance. The fields were full of them. They dotted the plains and stood on the ridges in the mountains afar. They overcame the scenery that was there before and became the scenery. But there was one place that remained empty, and that was the sky. I stared and stared at it for the longest time, knowing what I should do but was hesitant to do so. Finally, I took a deep breath and looked down at my hands and found the same palms, the same finger prints, the same lines, the same nails. I looked into the eyes of the first person I met, and realized that I was staring into my own eyes. I am it and it is me. We are all the same person, experiencing different places at different times, living different lives. However, we are still one and the same. I see myself looking back at me, I see myself looking up at me, and I see myself looking back down at me. I am everyone.

Everyone is me. We have differences in perspective, different pasts that we can all remember, but we are here together in this moment. I knew what they were thinking, they knew what I was thinking, and yet we are separate. If I choose to, I can make myself ignorant of their thoughts, and if I choose to, I can know everything about them from the moment they were born to the person they are now. Because we are all one. Whatever it was, be it a god or a devil, made us that way. Made me. This is what we are, and it is a principal part of our nature.

Then I blinked.

***

There I am, floating. There I was, floating. I was floating on my back in an endless indoor swimming pool at a recreation center of some sort when the lights were turned off. There was no one here, and only a gentle back and forth wave that echoed when it met the smooth walls of the pool. The blue moonlight poured in through the windows, painting the water in rippling lines of varied hues and tones. There was a deep stench of chlorine in the air mixed in with the humid atmosphere. I felt as though my entire body and I were one entity where I knew when my heart would beat, how my blood would flow, and when I would take each breath. I felt truly at peace which is something I had not known for a long time. Will there come a time when I can no longer experience this feeling?

I could sense my feet begin to drop below the surface, and noticed that there was a dark dye-like substance flowing gradually from my wrists. Blood, thick and moderately viscous. Yes, this was me trying to escape. Trying to die. Was this part of my imagination, or is this a memory? Is this happening, did it already happen, or did it never happen at all? Did the distinction matter anymore when it is all in my head regardless? I tried to remember whose memories these were. Out of eight billion people, it can be hard to pinpoint who you are when you are everyone. Yes, I remember now. This part of me was a teenaged swimmer, a talented one with potential who could no longer compete. The potential that was so deeply cherished had been dashed. What terrible luck! If only he started a little bit earlier, he may have been able to experience death instead of joining the rest of humanity in its current existence. The roll of the dice has been unkind. Fate had no mercy. My body no longer exists, this version of me no longer exists, and yet this moment feels so real to me just as it did during the time it happened. My knees followed, as the water poured over me. My head began to submerge, following my chest. The cold poured over me, inside and out. As I sank, I could see trails of darkness following after me, my colorless dark blood painting the streaks of flowing glimmers from the window in varying shades, like a rainbow of shadows spreading across my vision, until all I could see was black, bringing me back.

I faded back to the present to my current world of black and silence. In this expanse of cold and darkness dotted by celestial bodies lightyears away in the distance, I remembered once more: that feeling may have been real at one point, but it will never be real again outside the confines of my mind.

CHAPTER 3: THE STELLIFEROUS ERA

We are now witness to the Stelliferous Era which is the successor of the Primordial Era. This era marks the period where stars were born in the expanding vacuum known as the universe. It is during this time that the earth gave birth to life and eventually humans. The inflationary movements that began in the Primordial Era, directly following the Big Bang, are still continuing with increasing speed to this day with no sign of slowing. This initial era, lasting approximately one million Earth years, set the foundations of matter and energy upon which the Stelliferous Era and its many features could come into being over the following billions of years. Without the happenings of the Primordial Era, the stars we saw in our night skies would not exist, the planet we stood on would not exist, and we would not exist.

As though it was providence, the fundamental particles from this era eventually gave rise to the initial elements of hydrogen, helium, and lithium which formed the primary contents of the earliest stars known as population III stars. These comparatively massive and short-lived ancestors became the forge from which heavier elements such as carbon and some metals were generated, which would be seen in later generations of stars in the billions of years to come. The population II stars, which contained a higher concentration of heavier elements such as oxygen and some metals, while primarily containing lighter elements such as hydrogen and helium, succeeded the population III stars and are what form the halo of The Milky Way today. These are the older siblings of the more metal-heavy population I stars which form the disk of the galaxy and the oldest observable stars of the time. Population I stars define the modern age and it is one such star that humans called their home.

The solar system within which Earth is located is a collection of planetary bodies that revolve around the star that humans have called Sol after the Latin word for sun. These bodies, and the sun they revolve around were born from corpses of older stars with a finer pedigree of hydrogen and helium rather than the current mix of metals, semimetals, and nonmetals. After the birth of Sol, the matter that surrounded it began to revolve and coalesce into bodies of their own, becoming planetoids, and eventually planets. The scale of such planets ranged from thousands of miles to tens of thousands of miles in radius. For a human, this may be incomprehensibly large. However, it is quite small in comparison to the scale of the solar system which is at least five orders of magnitude larger with a radius in the billions of miles. When scaling out, the galaxy itself is far larger at a radius of hundreds of quadrillions of miles. While one can continue this exercise indefinitely until arriving at the observable universe of the time which is in the hundreds of sextillions of miles, even stopping at merely the solar system shows that the planets and bodies which humans called home is not even a speck in the vastness of the emptiness of creation. It should, of course, be noted that the observable universe does not represent the entirety of the universe itself, meaning that it is very much reasonable to say that affirming that Earth is not even a speck is an overstatement.

The rise of life itself is a more recent development that began with primitive microorganisms after the tumultuous formation of the Earth and its oceans. Initially starting with abiotically generated macromolecules that were capable of replication, this soon evolved into simple unicellular life capable of asexual reproduction. As environmental pressures determine which individuals died, and which individuals survived to reproduce, life gained greater complexity in its attempt to optimize its ability to survive and continue its legacy. Life became a self-sustaining algorithm whose main concern was one thing: its existence and continuation. Cellular life developed organelles and more sophisticated equipment by which to accomplish specialized tasks. Eventually, the acquisition and passing of traits through simple mutations became a bottleneck which necessitated methods that encouraged the capacity to escape from local maxima in terms of the highest level of individual fitness within a population. To illustrate this point, while an ax is ideal to chop down a tree, a butter knife may be sufficient. Life when armed with nothing more than mutations is doing nothing more than sharpening a butter knife when what it needs is an ax. But the ax would come and it would manifest in what would become the greatest source of genetic variability. This manifested in the form of sexual reproduction approximately two billion years prior to mankind's departure from the earth and allowed for a higher variety of traits within individuals by which a population is able to diversify.

The next revolution was that of multicellular life which permitted life to not only become larger in response to predation and environmental pressures, but also allowed for higher levels of redundancy such that losing a few cells here or there would not result in the death of the individual itself. Where a single cell may need to be able to respond to the environment as a whole, working in tandem with other cells enabled a level of cooperation such that responsibilities are split among the cells and higher levels of specialization can be achieved among the cells forming subcomponents of the whole in a way that is similar to organelles, but with a higher level of complexity and optimization. Simply put, each part of the body was primarily devoted to its role which allowed for the right tool to be used when needed. An ax for a tree, a hammer for a sword, skin cells for skin, white blood cells for immune responses, and many more.

Up to this point, animal life, which is a portion of complex multicellular life, was primarily confined to the sea. This changed, however, approximately 470 million years prior to the departure of mankind. The result was invertebrate and vertebrate species conquering the shifting, but empty, continents of the time and filling them with life. Amphibians became reptiles which then grew to dominate the earth. And then, as has been the case with each reshuffling of species, an extinction event occurred, wiping out three quarters of all species. This was a blow to life on Earth, but also an opportunity for others to fill in the empty spaces left by the dominant species of the time.

In addition to birds, mammals rose from the ashes of a battered Earth to take the place of the dinosaurs that ruled before them. Starting small and eventually growing in size, these warm blooded animals grew to dominate the earth and brought with them their own set of innovations. One such innovation was the development of a more sophisticated social structure that enabled improved coordination between individuals, leading to the success of the population. Like the unicellular cells before them, these individual units formed larger groups to improve their ability to generalize to a number of different environmental pressures from predators to famine, to large-scale disasters. Intelligence became a trait that emerged to allow for improved abilities to not only escape from predators, hunt down prey, and interact with others of the same species for better mating prospects, but also allowed for the use of tools as a way to overcome the limitations of the physical body to further exploit the environment to one's advantage. Among species that were capable of using tools, apes which diverged from other primates stood out as one of the more sophisticated, eventually evolving into humans that were capable of long distance travel, language, and high level reasoning.

These apes adopted a unique form of locomotion through bipedal movement that allowed for the free use of the forelimbs to use tools and a higher height to identify opportunities and threats far in the distance at the cost of speed. One foot could be placed in front of the other and with eyes facing front, the main direction that was considered was forward. By this point, the forward trajectory of humanity was set in stone. Progress had become the status quo. The toolmaking abilities allowed for inventions to propel the population of the species upwards. With Homo Erectus, who predated homo sapiens by more than a million years, came the use of fire which not only kept predators at bay, but also enabled cooking and advanced toolmaking. Fire was only the first domino in a long line of creations that continued till the end of humanity's tenure on Earth. Following the rise of Homo Sapiens, domestication and farming brought about the rise of settlements which transformed the lives of humans from hunter-gatherers to that of specialized settlers. There was a need for farmers, blacksmiths, masons, leaders, doctors, priests and scribes. All of whom served a specialized purpose within the larger collective. With the advent of writing which began as a method to track food stores and other resources, humans gained the capability of passing knowledge not only between generations, but also across centuries and after the fall of civilizations. Where humans could learn from previous generations before, with the advent of writing which persisted knowledge beyond human lifetimes, humans could now learn from previous civilizations, other cultures, and leave messages for their progeny long after their passing. Generations were able to build upon generations rather than starting from scratch. The human race and civilization by this point truly became a product of all of humanity rather than simply the living, making it the legacy of the whole race rather than mere individuals.

Materials advanced as well. First it was simple stone tools. However, stone eventually became bronze which was supplanted by iron. All the better to shape the world and kill one another with. The predators of the past were no longer a threat, and now, the largest threats were nature and other tribes and countries. Civilizations rose, fell, and were succeeded by those that learned from the mistakes of their predecessors. Systems of government changed from rudimentary forms of organization to sophisticated machines that attempted to better ensure the longevity of a society while sating the desires of the individuals within in order to maintain control.

Such control was disrupted by the need for information —a curiosity deeply ingrained within human nature. With the advent of the printing press, knowledge spread more quickly, enabling a larger population to not only gain information, but to disseminate it as well. This transformation impacted religion, scientific progress, and the frequency and speed at which news and information was updated. Such improvements in the dispersion of information was a boon to the scientific pursuits of the human race and soon led to advancements in an understanding of the laws of physics. Not only did Earth no longer stay the center of the universe, but the heavenly bodies, and the laws of motion were made clear. Humanity's place in the cosmos had become clearer and the fog was beginning to rise.

The applications of such concepts led to more refined tools capable of tremendously reducing human effort. With classical mechanics eventually leading to studies of energy, increased mastery of energy storage and transport ushered in a revolution in self-powered machines and the industrialization of many areas of commerce. Comprehension of electricity introduced instantaneous communication in the form of the telegraph as well as the transmission of energy over long distances. It is here that a dramatic shift in the transfer of knowledge can be seen. Previously, messages might take minutes to hours or even days to be sent and received, but the use of electric signals reduced the lag in communication by several orders of magnitude. This led to the beginning of a series of steps towards an optimizing of the computational aspects of society, and it was only a century afterwards that transistor based computers used similar techniques as the foundation for the far more sophisticated task of rapid calculation.

While computers were originally used for the purpose

of calculation, the concept of a programmable computer soon allowed for higher level operations beyond primitive calculations. This meant levels of abstraction beyond arithmetic and algebra, and the representation of more tangible items in a digital form. Mathematics and geometry became physics simulations which then led to user interfaces that acted as an intermediary between code understood by machines and actions understood by laypeople. The ability to represent almost anything in a digital format and present information in an understandable manner led to widespread adoption of the technology. This, combined with the ability to communicate digitally with a computer brought about a primitive representation of society's sea of consciousness which was called the internet. The internet became a playground for human activity, allowing for social interaction, while providing a wealth of data describing the intricacies of human behavior in great detail. Although it was originally accessed behind a computer screen, the internet eventually, for a moment, became an alternate reality that could be experienced as simply as breathing air through the use of neural interfaces that made all transactions occur at the speed of human thought. Within such an environment, prior to the last day man walked the earth, mankind began to run its finger along the seductive surface of human level general artificial intelligence. Just as mankind was about to attain the status of demigod by creating life with its own hands, it vanished from the surface of the earth, leaving behind a damaged planet with no appointed successors to its place. The legacy of humanity became like a mountain that ended in a sheer cliff and gradually weathered away leaving little trace.

Metal rusted. Concrete crumbled. Paint peeled. Wood foundations rotted. Power grids went offline. Buildings groaned and fell. Roads cracked to give way to plant life. Nature reclaimed the property of man with little fanfare. Knowledge disappeared as electricity no longer ran along the aging circuits and as paper decayed into detritus. It was an unceremonious end to the result of thousands of years of effort, and there was not even a single wail or cry to mark the tragic nature of a civilization's impact being whittled away.

The satellites and debris left behind in space stayed untouched indefinitely, with many objects eventually leaving orbit while others were unable to maintain it and ultimately entered the atmosphere. The global temperature's rate of increase slowed, but it did not stop the melting of glacial ice for many years. It was only until the sea levels have risen significantly to swallow the coastal lands that the earth began to truly heal. The turmoil brought upon by industry had vanished. In the absence of the continuous torture inflicted by the cruel ruler that unwillingly abdicated his throne, the earth and its biosphere was allowed a moment's rest. With its healing, perhaps there will be an opportunity for a more responsible steward to take the place of the civilizations that plundered the earth in the past.

CHAPTER 4: A WAY OUT?

"Do you know what year it is, or how long it has been since we have been trapped in this form?" the politician asked.

"I lost count after about twelve," a voice replied from deep within. "I don't think we age anymore. Does it still matter?"

Perhaps, I did still age. Perhaps I did not. There was no mirror. I could not raise my hands to my eyes or scream in the darkness. All I had were the orbits of the planets to tell me of the passage of time. We stayed fixed in one place, never moving, never interacting with anything within the solar system. We did not revolve around a large body, and only rotated approximately a degree every five minutes or so. Each year, we were given a close glimpse of the planet we once called home as it crossed our field of vision and then left. The first day, all the lights could still be seen on the earth. Afterwards, it was complete darkness. I could still make out manmade features, but it was clear that no one was home. If I knew the predicament I was in rather than simply denying it, perhaps we would have savored the sight I saw on that first day even more. Rather than wallow in disorientation, we could have lived in the moment, assuming that I am still living.

"Is this hell?" a child asked.

"It must be," a devout voice answered. "Even though we were forgiven for our sins, that didn't absolve us of our responsibilities as God's creations. We have sinned and this is our punishment."

"Then who among us is most guilty?" a preacher boomed through the emptiness of space. "Who is the one who has doomed us to this fate?"

An interesting question. Was it the soldiers that fought the wars? No. They were the greatest patriots. Was it the serial killers and mass murderers? Perhaps, but they were a misguided product of their society. Who among me has created those parts of me? Mediocre parents, abusive teachers, gun manufacturers, war hungry leaders, human traffickers, drug dealers, exploitative employers, dishonest journalists, pedophiles, rapists, the authority, the elite, the vagrants. All are part of me. All of them are me. I am as guilty as I am innocent. The generation before us made us flaws and imperfections, and left us here to suffer while they could enjoy death and freedom from this form of existence. They left without even a sense of shame of the wrongdoings they have committed and left us here as scapegoats for crimes committed throughout the entire history of the human race. Who do I burn at the stake now that we're here like this? Who can I throw off a roof, stone, hang, and behead? Where is the pike for me to parade the heads of the villains who created this outcome? And who among me is most befitting of the role of executioner? I doubt there is even one among me that is without sin, who can cast the first stone, raise the ax, and load the bullets for the firing squad.

I hate so much of myself for conflicting reasons. All the imperfect and flawed individuals, no matter how high of an office or low of a position they held were me. All of them fill me with a deep sense of loathing that makes me want to tear myself apart out of pure aversion and ego due to the notion that I am even remotely related to anyone else. I hate those of a certain race, and I also hate those of all the other races. I hate the capitalists and I also hate the communists. I hate the men, the women, the children, and everyone in between. I hate those who are citizens of the United States, and I also hate those who are citizens of Russia. I hate one side of me, and the side I hate despises the others. The ones on the other side are the ones responsible. They are the ones who should be punished. They are the ones who deserve this. Don't lump them in with us. Or else we, all sides, all of me, will never find peace.

If I can bring them to justice maybe then, I can earn an escape from this reality. Quid pro quo. I punish myself, and by doing so, free myself. We would do anything, give anything, in exchange for our freedom. Tell us what you want. If we can, we will deliver.

I am the one pursued by the mob and I am the mob itself. Indeed, we have seen moments like this before—moments where we were placed on trial, judged for our crimes, regardless of guilt or innocence. The times I have been framed for a murder and separated from my children by the justice system. I stood there in a publicized court at the mercy of a judge and jury who knew nothing about me or what I had at stake and a disinterested public defender who was overburdened by the number of cases he needed to handle. Even before the trial started, I was met with vitriol and disgust. I learned then that in the court of public opinion, I was guilty until proven innocent. There, in that sterile environment, I had no one I could call a friend who could save me in my time of need. I was being watched by everyone, scrutinized, and judged with little say in the matter. Everyone wanted something from me except the things I wanted. The zealous prosecutor wanted the death penalty. He and his team fought tooth and nail ensure that I get nothing, not even a morsel. He fought for death, but I was given life in prison instead as though it was supposed to be some form of mercy. The reasoning was that the severity of the crime notwithstanding, my financial situation and my gender did not warrant an execution. I was privileged enough to avoid death, but lacking enough privilege to avoid a life of intense suffering. The humiliation I felt at that point was unbearable, as though I truly wished to repent for a crime I did not commit. It was then that I realized that justice was fickle, and that truth, regardless of its value, only had meaning when it was revealed. My faith in the systems I was once told to believe in had been demolished.

In the days following the trial, I was immediately sent to a high security prison without even given the chance to see my family or protest the decision in any way. I did nothing wrong, but I was being punished. My identity was overtaken by my sentence. My education, my past accomplishments, all the good I have done was replaced by what a court incorrectly decided I was. My fellow prisoners were violent criminals, willing to commit crime at a moment's notice. When the prison guards were not there to torment me, those who were in the same position that I was decided to take the opportunity to do so themselves. Whether it be through boredom, an unwarranted enmity, or self-hatred, those around me turned against me. However, those moments were in the minority as I spent the majority of my time in a cell, watching an unchanging scenery from behind a set of bars. Trapped 'til death do us part.

"There's no need to count the years," an astronomer said. "The stars can tell us exactly how long it has been."

Astronomical dating. It is a possibility. But I am merely an accumulation of all humans in the form of a single individual. I have all my senses, but I do not appear to have a human body. My vision is that of a human's. My hearing, if it worked in this empty vacuum, is most likely the same. There is no air here, but if I could smell, what scent would I recognize? Taste? Not even worth mentioning. If I could speak, even if someone could hear me, what could I say? The stars in the distance were dim and did not twinkle. There was no telescope here. No technology or tools. Nothing can be made, and nothing can be used except for my mind. Physical autonomy was a thing of the past. Sometimes, I would catch a comet or planetary bodies in the form of colored dots when the sun was behind me. It was a rough guess, but we think that it has been almost a century.

A century of nothing. I have eyes but I cannot close them. I long for sleep, but have no need to. And with the absence of sleep is also the absence of dreams which was one of my primary escapes before I became... this. Now, the only escapes are the memories of billions and my imagination which serves not only to occasionally free me, but also tortures me incessantly as it did when I walked the earth as many instead of one. My sight acts not only as a reminder of the state we are in, but also as the source of infinite boredom as I spin and spin. The days blend into weeks, which become years and decades. Time passes slowly, but the time that has passed seems so very dull due to there being no significant or meaningful memories over the years. It is all one blur of inactivity, anxious thought, and monotony.

I have these memories of lives with gaps, empty spaces, and blanks. Lives that ended in accidents and injuries, but still lived to become a part of me. From the outside, I can see nurses and doctors act as witness to the events that occurred during these blanks. Wires everywhere leading from bodies to monitors. Intravenous catheters to deliver nutrients to my emaciated body while I lay there on a hospital bed unaware of the happenings of the world. Maybe it was for the best. If I could see myself, injured, burnt, scarred, and unconscious, I would have asked to pull the plug. Now, I see myself wishing that there was a plug. Yes, I can see the entirety of existence for what it is, but at what cost? Even if I did recover and woke up, there was no normal life waiting for me at the end of all the time that had passed. To see myself, old and decrepit, with my youth robbed from me. To see the world move on without me and leave me behind. How different would that be from this? Those among me that were unconscious were fortunate. When I was conscious, but unable to communicate, it was as though reality was ridiculing me. Telling me that it placed me on that hospital bed to allow me to see my own funeral as my family and loved ones fought over whether I lived or died.

I remember wishing that someone, anyone, would help me. That if they could not save me, they would reassure me. Now, if anyone is to save me, they would be light years away, maybe on another planet. They could be in another time in the far future, waiting to evolve into a form that had the intelligence and capabilities to take to the stars. Someone please... No one will save me. I'm not a princess in a fairytale. The only one who can save me is myself if such a thing is possible. But we can't save ourselves. We don't know how.

My eyes cannot weep. If I had a mouth, my sobs would be

lost in this blackness. If I had a heart, its aches would not even register. Nothing can save me from this misery that I cannot even feel. We are at the mercy of the cosmos, its scale, and its pace. If there is a way out, it would take lifetimes, millennia, and epochs of time. No longer do I operate in the world of the living. I am now peer to the planets, stars and galaxies, waiting for salvation on a cosmological timescale extending almost infinitely into an unknown future. I can only hope that before the universe ends, I, all of us, have a chance at a real life once more, or at least a merciful death.

This is our reality now, whether I like it or not. To live, fixed to a single point in the universe, unable to physically interact with anything, to have my individuality taken away and melded into a monstrosity that is the entirety of humanity, the embodiment of society as a single individual. Privacy, identity, a sense of self. All are gone now.

There is only me, Humanity, left to shoulder the future burdens of the race that came before me regardless of whether I am able to do so or not.

CHAPTER 5: FREAKSHOW

When we sent out the first of our interstellar probes in the year 3121 of the Stellar calendar era to visit our stellar neighbor, we believed what we now call the Anomaly to be a moon or satellite due to the low resolution of the images that were captured and the speed at which our probe was traveling at the time. At the time, we did not notice much about it other than its peculiar location. Typically, smaller objects are swept up within the gravitational well of the larger bodies close by. This usually includes planets, or the star itself. The prospect of something akin to the Anomaly being positioned where it was within the solar system was probabilistically low beyond any margin of error. It was as though it was placed there, and even if it was not, the series of events that led to its current state were beyond simple explanation.

A primarily stationary object is definitely unique indeed and was a slight point of interest among our scientists on the first pass. Of course, it was nothing in comparison to the unique chemical composition of the fourth or third planet which may serve as points of settlement for future colonies. The third in particular had indications that its atmosphere was generated through more than simple chemical processes which led us to postulate that there was the potential for carbon based life forms that use nitrogen, oxygen, water, and carbon to survive. However, while these developments were exciting, the information passed back to us from our first probe was limited as a majority of the onboard equipment was dedicated to the acceleration and shielding of the probe itself. We needed to use pattern recognition techniques and machine learning to take an image that was captured at a quarter of the speed of light and turn it into information that we could understand. The machine learning models we utilized were generated by using the data we collected in prior missions that were directed towards areas that we have sent probes to in the past and comparing them with missions that were not at quite the same speed or with images collected through space telescopes. Turning a blur into a legible image was extremely difficult, and we could only really make imperfect approximations that were later refined by probes 2 and 3.

Probe 2 was launched immediately after the first probe with the intention of capturing the solar system from a different angle at a slower speed using a different set of instrumentation and sensors. Since propulsion and speed was less of a concern with the second pass, we were not only able to take clearer images, but also increase the payload on the probe to allow for a higher number of sensors to collect more information. Unlike probe 1 which used a primarily photonic based form of propulsion, probe 2 used a combination of nuclear and photonic propulsion and gravity to slingshot itself towards the solar system along a slightly different trajectory. This made it a more economical project that could provide more data in exchange for a longer travel time. If probe 1 was a bullet, probe 2 was an arrow. Each served their own purpose in unveiling the mystery that is the cosmos. Upon reaching the solar system, we could gain a better understanding of the number of planets, and its general organization. In addition to this, we could better track the movement of the Anomaly and confirm its trajectory. Previously, it was as though we only knew that there was gold in a general area. With probe 2, we understood where to dig. This planet-like structure rotates periodically, and moves through space in a straight line at a speed that exponentially increases. Whether its velocity is increasing exponentially or along an s-curve was still to be determined at this point. Clearly, it did not exert the force of gravity, nor was it affected by gravity. Whether it was able to physically interact with other objects or had mass was questionable as well despite its physical appearance. It clearly reflected light, and could be seen along multiple wavelengths of the electromagnetic spectrum, but other properties did not follow the laws of physics that we were aware of up to that point. Our researchers speculated whether it was made of something other than normal matter and follows some laws of physics while ignoring others. There was also a question of what its top speed and starting velocity was, and whether the current speed of this object can be used to determine where it started and its relative age. If we had here an object that could upend our knowledge of the laws of physics, the study of it would likely result in large advancements in our science and technology. Here was something that was an answer to questions we asked in the past and those we had yet to ask. It was as though we had the answer key to a textbook full of questions that would absolutely disrupt our ways of thinking. However, answers alone were not enough to reverse engineer the question. We needed more answers and seeing how it was in our interest to eventually establish colonies, further information was needed prior to sending crewed missions and generation ships. A case was made, and the appropriate funding was given for the improvement of existing space travel methods as well as the development of alternate forms of interstellar travel that could be used to reduce the number of probes that needed to be sent in the long term and increase the speed at which these long journeys needed to be completed.

In the year 3138, Probe 3 adopted a trajectory that took advantage of an alignment of four bodies: the anomaly, the third planet and its moon, and the fourth planet. This allowed for the probe to perform a flyby which could approach more closely and view each body in succession. The fourth planet held an atmosphere with properties similar to ours despite being thinner and seemingly devoid of life. Its atmosphere indicated that it held a dying electromagnetic field which meant that while the planet was prime for terraforming into a form that complemented our biology, doing so would be time consuming and an uphill battle. It was believed that we could perhaps consider bioengineering ourselves instead, but that was a consideration for a later time when we began construction of the first generation ships. Prior to doing so, however, were the landers and orbiters that would not only provide more detailed analyses on a constant basis, but also a less surface level (pun intended) understanding of the planets and the Anomaly itself.

The Anomaly's chemical composition was fascinating, but did not inform us of how it was able to treat gravity as though it was nonexistent. The planetoid seemed to consist of oxygen, carbon, hydrogen, and nitrogen. This matched quite well with the chemical composition of the third planet's atmosphere. In trace amounts were other elements such as calcium, phosphorus, potassium, and sulfur. Through molecular spectroscopy, we could observe that there was a high presence of water, proteins, and lipids which exceeded any margin of error. We had an idea of what to expect through the use of space telescopes, but the resolution and clarity of information was disappointing when compared to the quality of information provided by the probe. The high amount of water was interesting, but the high level of proteins and lipids indicated that perhaps this object was organic which was very bizarre. It is one thing for a large body to contain traces of organic matter. It is another thing for the body itself to be organic. The fringe of the scientific community posited that this was a living being or a colony of living beings that was originally formed on the third planet or constructed in space using resources originating from the third planet. If so, approaching the object could be considered first contact. While first contact may be a landmark in the advancement of our species and a milestone that we never believed to have reached this early, we needed confirmation as there were many questions such a conclusion may bring. How did this object enter space if it was organic? If it is a form of life, was it simple or intelligent? Could we communicate with it? Conversely, would we want to communicate with it if we could?

The last question in particular was of interest to military organizations and led to an ice age in our exploration of the solar system for many decades. We did not know what it was, and as a result, lacked the ability to determine if it constituted a danger or not. If we were in a situation where we were technologically inferior to any life out there, we were unable to know. Similarly, we limited electromagnetic communications to within our own solar system so as to avoid alerting any malicious actors of our presence while hoping that the probes sent out on previous missions went by unnoticed. Our civilization entered into a cold war with life forms that were hypothetically out there and focused on the advance of technology so as to place ourselves within the best position to counter any threats. It was a position driven by a fear of the unknown. The age was one of flight despite not knowing if there was a fight to be had. We continued to research propulsion, physics, and improved our observational powers by placing telescopes and sensors on the edge of our solar system. It was a conversation where we were always listening, but never answering back and did not know who was speaking. The whole of our civilization, colonies and home planet included, entered into a shadow boxing match where any possibility and any assumptions of technological inferiority were considered to waterproof our defenses against the outside.

We began by preparing for the typical attacks we may have faced: nuclear, biological, kinetic, etc. Once these were resolved, we considered informational vectors. Cyber-attacks, propaganda, mind viruses, rogue artificial intelligences and the like were carefully reviewed. In the process, our information technology and our understanding of mathematics grew by leaps and bounds. This helped us to plan against attacks beyond our understanding of the laws of physics. Temporal attacks, attacks from other dimensions, and the use of parallel realities as a playground to strategize against the enemy. We did not fully master these concepts, but we did develop strategies to recognize when such attacks would be launched against us, and how to respond accordingly. This was as far as we could go.

Our curiosity and public sentiment could not be held back by fear anymore. Our people were descended from explorers and pioneers. We were meant to be out there, not to hide in the shadows. We could no longer fight against our nature. This is of course merely an excuse. Civil unrest and economic weakness meant that a distraction was needed. All the cards were already collected and our leadership knew what hand to play. Facing violent protests and the threat of civil war, we made the decision to resume exploration and potentially enter a new era for our species, or risk its potential destruction by continuing on this path.

Many decades after we sent our last probe, in the year 3196 of the Stellar calendar era, the Trinity project was the next step we would take prior to sending out generation ships. This project consisted of three probes— each of which was a lander and an orbiter that would allow for high resolution mapping of the ground from orbit and physical analysis of the surface in multiple frequencies and spectra. These probes were meticulously constructed works of shining art that utilized the latest advances in material science, manufacturing, and logistics. From an economic standpoint, each government was mobilized to spare some level of effort towards this undertaking. For each probe, the majority of the mass was that of an engine whose purpose was primarily to decelerate the probe for the majority of its journey towards its target. Where in prior missions, shuttles and ships were unable to provide high amounts of useful data due to the speed at which they traveled, the change in focus from acceleration to deceleration provided a way to use light speed travel to gain the needed speed, but also reach appropriate velocities needed for orbital missions. The method of travel used within the Trinity project was as follows: the probes utilized a light sail pushed by a photonic array to accelerate to their top speed. Upon reaching their top speed, they immediately decelerate using rudimentary and somewhat experimental antimatter based propulsion to shave down the speed on its century long journey. Upon approach to the solar system of the targets, the probes will detach their antimatter engines and then use nuclear fusion and ion engines for the remainder of their travel to their destination.

This was the sequence of events that were to be performed, and for each milestone, the generations that were there at the beginning, and the generations that succeeded them watched in suspense waiting for anything to go wrong with the complex machinery. It was centuries of high tension where all who stood at the forefront of the mission were on constant edge due to the complexity of the maneuvers, but also the pressure from bureaucracy to not screw up and set a negative precedent that jeopardizes any future missions. Fortunately, each stage, from the assembly of the orbiters and landers in zero gravity to the firing of the photonic array to the ignition and detachment of the antimatter engine occurred satisfactorily without much deviance from previously run simulations. In other words, operating conditions were optimal, and at the end of a century of waiting, in the year 3303 of the Stellar calendar era, we were at the end of our limited supply of patience. It was the time for answers.

The second probe, the name of which roughly translates to "divine stone" in the most commonly spoken language of our civilization, was the first to enter orbit around the third planet. On entering orbit, it was met with a fair amount of debris which it needed to navigate around to avoid any damages. Analysis of this debris showed a number of shapes and features such as straight edges and right angles that occurred at a frequency that was well above that which may be considered naturally occurring. It is highly likely that all of these pieces were artificially made, and that they may have once been part of the same object in the past. There is an abundance of plastics and carbon based compounds that we have never found to have been formed naturally up to this point during our exploration of the galaxy up to this point. The simplest explanation is that these objects are the remnants of intelligent life that was capable of space travel.

The lander only confirmed our suspicions once it separated from the orbiter and began its mission. Down at ground level, we found remnants of large cities which have been overtaken by vegetation in the form of secondary ecological succession. Not only is there life here, but it is thriving, and it gave birth to creatures capable of manipulating their environment and mastering it. The existence of this single planet has given credibility to the field of astrobiology and formed extensions of the existing fields of paleontology, anthropology, sociology and others by adding the dimension of extraterrestrial civilizations. The Divine Stone lander which was capable of aerial, land, and underwater travel managed to cover significant ground in an autonomous manner and was able to show us the extent of life and the ruined civilization's progress from the way their land was utilized to multiple writing systems to their physical bipedal form which was shown to us in the form of statues and illustrations. Time would be needed to decode their languages, but one question was at the forefront of all others and that was why these intelligent beings which seemed to be capable of space travel abandoned their planet when it was obvious that it was not under any significant crisis. Core samples taken at the northernmost pole indicated an increase in greenhouse gasses. While a significant change in environmental conditions could indeed affect biodiversity and the like, that was not enough to explain why cities of such size did not have the remains of a population to match. It is unlikely that these beings were unable to utilize their technology and progress to solve such problems, so the prevailing theory was not that they were wiped out, but rather that they left. As to why, perhaps the other orbiters could shed light on this mystery while the Divine Stone lander continued its investigation autonomously.

The first probe which was named Eternal Forge after an item from an ancient religion many millennia ago arrived at the fourth planet to find similar debris in orbit. However, the main difference is that such debris and satellites were in lesser quantities than the third planet. This indicated that the conditions for the intelligent life which lived within this solar system favored that of high levels of oxygen, nitrogen, and water. Perhaps this civilization was only just beginning to colonize its system as there is less of a presence of artifacts like the ones we found on the third planet. There were no large cities here, but rather small colonies which used dome structures to separate the planet's thin atmosphere from the artificial atmosphere that was sealed in. Those of us observing back on our home planet immediately began designs for missions to the moons of the third and fourth planet as it was likely that similar colonies could be found in those locations as well. Based on the waste products of these colonies, it appeared that methane, and solar power were used to power these facilities. While resourceful, compared to our current stage of technological advancement, it was quite elementary. There were some spaceships parked nearby which had designs suited for chemical propulsion which only reinforced our impression that this civilization had their progress cut short before they could reach their full potential. With this in mind, we looked towards the Anomaly and asked ourselves whether that thing was a creation of these people, or if it was the reason for their ruin. The latter led to us second guessing our decision, but by this point it was too late. The third probe had already reached its destination.

The third probe, named World Tree after a common motif in many religions of our past, was unable to enter into orbit around the Anomaly. The reason for this was because the Anomaly possessed no gravitational field. This meant that it needed to decelerate significantly more than the other probes to avoid flying away in the absence of the pull of gravity. Originally, we thought that due to the smaller size of the planetoid that it would have a lower gravitational pull, but the complete lack of gravity was a surprise even though this object appeared to defy the laws of physics. As the orbiter oriented itself towards the Anomaly, it became obvious that the lander could not be launched from the orbiter and needed to be placed on the surface. Until then, it was not a viable avenue for observation and exploration. Ignoring all laws of physics and common sense, the orbiter approached in a straight line. As the orbiter closed in, the discolored ball of organic matter gradually gained features. There were lines and bumps on the surface that did not appear to be the result of tectonics. While there is heat being emanated by the Anomaly, it was not quite what would be expected of a planetoid capable of volcanic activity. This was different. It acted more like a living organism with a core temperature.

Gaining proximity, the nature of this thing became clearer. There were tubule-like structures spanning the entirety of the sphere. It was as though it was a planet-sized mass of carbon based flesh with structures resembling blood vessels or capillaries spanning the surface. Upon reaching a distance of meters from the surface, those bumps which were observed before took on a recognizable shape. It was a shape that was observed on the surface of the third planet. These imprints were similar to that of the faces of the beings that once ruled the third planet, each contorted into hollowed out expressions. It was as though each of them were perpetually frozen in some emotion. Whether these were expressions of euphoria or horror was something we had yet to determine at that point due to gaps in our understanding of the social behaviors of those beings. When we studied the third planet, we suspected that the population of intelligent beings was somewhere in the billions if their infrastructure was any indication. When we took the small sample size of faces we found and extrapolated them to the entire surface of the Anomaly, our calculations indicated there were billions of them all over the sphere of organic matter. Did the jigsaw piece fit, or was it a red herring from another puzzle set? We left the lander to float towards the object, and upon contact, it just passed through as though it was not there.

We could not study it directly. We could not speak to it. We could not greet it. Simply put, we did not understand it. What was it? How old is it? Why did it exist? It could have been anything: the product of an intelligent civilization, a generation ship, a living being, a computer, an art installation, a shrine. We did not know, and at the time, we did not even remotely have the mindset nor the advancements needed to grasp what this was. It was only in the future as our civilization and our people changed that we understood that the mystery would haunt us and guide us on a journey across time, space, and realities where we would find that the thing we needed to understand most was ourselves. These first few centuries were nothing more than a warm up for the odyssey that was to come.

CHAPTER 6: THE ABSENT SELF

Go to school. Get high grades. Attend a reputable university. Find a good job. Find a spouse. Get married. Have children. Watch them grow. Retire. Live the last moments of your life in regret. Question whether you will be remembered by anyone after you are gone while knowing that your accomplishments were not unique in the slightest despite doing everything right. See yourself wither and die a mundane death. Rinse and repeat.

Be born. Struggle to eat. Go on living despite the pain it brings you. See the people around you starve and wander through despair as though it was an ordinary part of life. Die emaciated, diseased, and alone, wondering why you had to suffer so. Rinse and repeat.

Live in peace without offending anyone. Watch as your lands are overrun by foreigners and razed to the ground because you do not speak the right language or worship the same god. Lose your limbs to an explosive device. Ask what sins you have committed to deserve this fate. Dream of the feeling of having your hands and feet shredded and feel the pain— the pain that you felt on the day you had your former life taken away from you. Learn that in another country, in another land more blessed than yours, you could have kept your hands. Realize that the monetary value of your life is lower than others in the world. Die asking why we are born unequal, live unequally, and die unequally. We are all the same outside the realm of the living, but so different from one another within life. Rinse and repeat.

"It never ends does it? No matter where we live or what we do, it never ends. We live and afterwards, it is as though we were never here," a sole voice shouted within the masses.

We have reached the verge of death many times, and have questioned countless times why we were alive, why we continued to live in the face of unfair and cruel circumstances. What is it that matters, especially now that civilization is lost to the past? In many past lives, I have worked and worked and worked. Sometimes to simply live. Other times for material possessions which had little meaning and only became devalued with the passage of time. We have led many lives which revolved around meaningless items which lacked any functionality other than to represent value. We said, "This piece of paper has value. It has this much value. Here is what you can exchange it for." Later, we said, "These bytes have value. It is equivalent to this much of our favorite piece of paper." It did not matter the face on the piece of paper, the color of the piece of paper, which computer calculated which blocks on the chain, or the amount of energy used in the calculation. As long as we agreed that it had value and we reached a consensus on how much, people were willing to exchange their time for it, to kill others over it, and to ruin their lives for it. Now, there is no such thing. What do I live for now?

"You do it to live. You do it to justify your place in society," an executive said.

None of that applies anymore. There is no society, and no one is asking for me to justify my place in the universe. I have nothing to prove. Gone is the footing I had. Now, for better or worse, it is all up to us.

Humans have certain needs. I had certain needs. Food, water, shelter. None of these apply anymore. I feel no hunger, and have no thirst. While in the past, these factors were motivators, now, I wish I felt at least those impulses. Cravings to eat something. A cold drink in hot weather. Sexual urges. An escape from pain. I feel nothing now. My body has become impeccably immune to the pressures of the outside, but in gaining such an advantage, we have lost so much of what makes us who we are. No carrot, and no stick. There is nothing to work for, and nothing to flee from. There is merely a cavern of missing emotions and feelings in the place where human experience once was. There is no constant drive for productivity anymore. No quarterly deadlines. No crops to tend to. No laws to pass. No people to save. No reputation to uphold. No one to exploit. No one to be exploited by. No one to please. No family to support. No materials to buy. No high end car to buy and show off. There's only one fancy car floating out here in space, and I don't have the hands to grab the steering wheel.

"This is freedom isn't it?" a part of me asked. "Isn't this what we always wanted?"

In a sense, it is the ultimate freedom, but what can I do with this freedom? I feel nothing bad, but conversely, I feel nothing good. As though I am locked within a sensory deprivation tank and someone threw away the keys. Physical pain is no longer real, but I still hurt all the time. It's just in our head. Every time I try to blink myself out of this horrific daydream, every time I am reminded of what I've become, I feel a sharp burning that I know is not there. And then I become afflicted with a yearning for something like the old times. I look back upon the times when I cut myself with a twisted nostalgia. Oh how I wish we could do that to ourselves one more time. As though it is right, as though it would allow for me to escape this fate by bartering for my future with my current agony. Give me a whip and I will whip myself till there is nothing but crimson and sinew showing. Give me a match and a can of gasoline and I will set myself on fire. Give me a cross to bear and I will gladly nail myself to it. I know it won't be enough, but give me a chance. Give me a chance to feel something again. Give us our punishment. Give me a way out.

"Who are you speaking for? I don't want to die quite yet."

"The majority of course. The dominant thoughts win out. Although, sometimes, it's those nagging thoughts that grow like a parasite to eventually overpower the mundane ideas of the human mind."

Let me kill myself. Let me end it. At least allow us the choice. Unlike those times when we had a second thought, I promise I will succeed this time. I will not hesitate. We can end it right now. Just give us a chance. Be it a nuclear bomb, a gun to the head, a fall from a bridge, an artificially produced disease, or self-imposed genocide, I am ready and fully willing. No longer will I be a burden to others, to our planet, to the universe. No longer will we be a drain on a society that no longer exists. To repent for the wickedness of occupying this space, I will perform the ultimate act of courage and end it all. I plead guilty your honor and I ask for the death penalty. We no longer wish for this perverse liberty. I want death…

But there is no guarantee that even if I plead with the heart and soul of billions that there is someone out there listening. We don't know if this was the result of someone, or a naturally occurring freak accident where the odds simply did not play out in our favor. What has happened, happened; leaving me here in an existence that is paradoxical when compared to our previous one. What is the point now? What do I live for? Why do I continue to exist? All I fear now is that each second, minute, and day will come and I will still be there to see it. I dread each moment that passes, but I fear nothing else. I once used to dread our mortality. Each moment I thought of it, I would immediately think of anything else so as to avoid wasting my time fearing something that was inevitable. I did everything to distract myself with the truth by immersing myself in life and lying for a lifetime. And everyone, all of me, did the same, not thinking of the end too frequently lest they be frozen and miss the moments they believed truly mattered. Everybody asked the question, but no one could provide a convincing answer. What does it mean to live all this life only to die? Were all my actions meaningless if we were only going to die in the end?

"No, that can't be right. Even if what we do does not last, doesn't it mean something if we lived at all?" a part of me spoke up.

"Says who?" another replied.

How did I live with my mortality hanging over me? I distracted myself with other things. I convinced myself life had a purpose despite there being no such evidence for such a thing beyond evolutionary needs. I would fabricate the most unlikely reasons when Occam's razor suggests that the simplest explanation is the most likely. There is no purpose to life. There is no meaning beyond the meaning that we create ourselves and by doing so lie in the process. The more I think of it, the more I realize how bleak our tiny existence was. I will die. My children will die. Their children will die, and with each generation, I will gradually become forgotten and lost to time as though I never existed. Civilizations will collapse. The planet I was born on will no longer exist. This star I revolved around will no longer exist and with it, the solar system is stardust once more. The life I lived would change nothing, and mean nothing.

But what about now? Has anything changed now that I have become everlasting? I know the predictions of what will happen to this solar system, the galaxy, and the observable universe. What once was a mortal life on an insignificant dot in an ocean of nothing has merely become an immortal life in an apathetic reality that could not care less whether we were here or not. We were alone then, clinging to our island in this hostile emptiness, and we are alone now. Is there other life out there? I think it is a possibility. But if anyone is out there and trying to communicate, they can't hear us, and we can't reply back. We can send letters, but they will only get lost on their way to addresses that do not exist. There was a probe, but it later lost power and floated away into the distance. If that was first contact, it was underwhelming to say the least. No handshake, no conversation, no glance of approval. No hello, and no goodbye. Just cold hard metal meeting with whatever it is I have metamorphosed into. Like ships passing at sea.

It is like those moments when I sat alone by the window of many apartment rooms all across the world, grimy and stained by water spots, watching the world outside. I would have the curtains partially closed while I glanced outside, wondering if I should leave my room, but find a reason not to. Be it laziness, anxiety, or a general dislike of other people, I imposed upon myself a loneliness by forcing my view of the outside to be from the limited portal of a glass frame. If I could have simply stepped outside and walked down there, I too could have lived a life like everyone else. Maybe I could have had an education and widened my horizons. Maybe I could have met others, started relationships, and grown in the process. A simple hello could have been all I needed. Perhaps I could have become a completely different person with a more fulfilling set of events to look back upon in old age. Instead I chose a cheap imitation of reality, preferring the virtual to the real to avoid any confrontation or additional effort. Convenience over satisfaction. The possibilities that could have been are lost in the spaces we never traversed.

We lived in a world that had no necessity for human contact, and human relations could be disposed of in some instances. The food I ate, the supplies I needed, all could be procured without needing to take one step outside. There is an app to take away the work under the guise of convenience while also taking away interaction as we know it. Everything can be mailed or delivered. The bland microwaveable food I unwillingly consumed daily had a taste that you would think was only meant for astronauts or the poorest of souls. Just take your frozen muck with its horrid consistency, stick it in a machine that hums for two minutes and you have your heated muck with the nutritional value of cardboard. The flavor was demoralizing. It was food that was only suited for those who had very little respect for themselves— basically everyone or at least a large percentage of the country. As days turned to weeks within these darkened rooms, I would watch my body atrophy and turn into a perverted joke of what I once was. The months turned to weeks. I was nothing more than an aging body wasting its youth. One the few times I needed to meet someone with the door, the moments were brief, and the eye contact was minimal. It was as though I never saw them, and we never met. We were both lost in our own words— him in his work and I in my mind. Whenever given a chance to act, I choose inaction. Days pass, and I dread each day and struggle to leave my bed, wishing that I never woke up. I wanted nothing more than for the days to pass, and at the same time, I hated each wasted moment and blamed myself for it. A fear of failure stayed my hand, which made me idle. My idleness directed my bitterness towards myself at the end of each day, and as I go to sleep, all I can say is that tomorrow might be better with nothing of substance to support it. The cycle of misery continued.

I see a text on my smartphone and it is a friend who I did not have much contact with since I graduated from university. I ignore it and instead opt to chat online with strangers. It is a world that is quite easy to get lost in. So much so that even when there was a hand I could grasp to pull me out, I refused it. There were those in this world of text and URLs who engaged in conversation without any ulterior motives while there were others who spoke provocatively so as to elicit extreme reactions for their own entertainment. If you fell for their trap, you may have found yourself lost within a sea of bitterness and outrage over the most mundane concepts or even illusory topics that have been constructed primarily for the purpose of having something to be angry about. Be it the government, certain politicians, petty squabbles over fashion, income, race and sexuality, or generational divides, there is something for everyone to find themselves overly invested in that they ultimately have no power or control over in any significant way. For many with some marginal level of self-awareness, there is a moment of clarity between these phases of emotional outbursts on the internet where one questions why they wasted their time on something so pointless. The person on the other end may not even be acting on good faith. They could be an individual who is acting on the behalf of another country to spread disinformation. Similarly, they could not be human.

It was a problem that we experienced towards the end of our civilization: differentiating between one of us, and bots which were capable of convincingly human conversations. The idea that we were arguing with something we ourselves constructed was an unsettling thought, and only served to exacerbate the disappointing weight of our condition— that we were depriving ourselves of a human life, and replacing it with an artificial one with artificial friends and individuals. It very much could have been that none of the experiences we had that were meaningful were real. The information we were given was not experienced by ourselves first hand. We never met the people on the other side of the LED screen. Not much different from our current predicament is it not?

It brings us to question what we see. All of it. "Is anything I am seeing real?"

"Look for clues. If it is not real, then there should be inconsistencies. A human mind is an imperfect one," a neurologist spoke out.

Indeed, it is hard to say. We could be dreaming it. Similarly, how do we know that we are not an artificial creation much like those bots that so many versions of me were tricked into interacting with unknowingly? What is the difference? I see this solar system, the planets that I remember living on. However, none of those facets of my experience could necessarily be real. My memories are that of billions, and my experience is not a human one. Perhaps humanity reached a point where it was not only able to simulate a human brain, but also intelligences orders of magnitude more complex. I may simply be an experiment in a long line of advancements to not only reproduce human level intelligence, but to also go beyond. What is the utility in giving a single individual with a human level intelligence the memories of many people? I do not know. Perhaps it is to see if I arrive at an identity. To see if I have a sense of self, or if I wander through life confused and lost within the memories that I was programmed to have. Maybe it is to see if I have one personality or multiple. To see how volatile I am.

Maybe it is a way to skirt the ethical quandaries faced during human experimentation. Perhaps that is why they needed me, to see how a human might act if they live longer lives, or can download the memories of others without limit. If so, then there may indeed be an end to this never-ending experience. Maybe once I reach the end of the universe, those on the outside will pull the plug. Is that a light at the end of the tunnel, or a great disappointment? Maybe I wished deep inside that I was human, that these memories and the strong feelings I recollect from them were real and meant more to me.

"Is there a way for me to know for sure? A conclusive method to determine what is real and what is not?"

"Construct a hypothesis. See what we can observe, and if our observations don't match, then the hypothesis is false. We need to collect empirical data and draw our conclusions. Science is our only ally."

I don't know if I am truly here. Past a perfect asteroid belt, nearing the orbit of a pristine and turbulent Jupiter, I have no way of understanding what "here" actually is. But I am a thinking entity capable of having a sense of self. It's a start, but even if I know that, what are our options? I have my senses. I can see. I have a sense of balance. It would seem illogical to only have those senses, so I should have my hearing, smell, and touch as well. With that said, I feel no pain, and other than the acknowledgement that it is cold, it is impossible to determine if I have a sense of touch. If I have a body, a physical body, the absence of sensation on my skin and pain place me in the interesting situation where I cannot experience what it is like to have a body. In the absence of pain, the absence of your physical self also seems to fade away. With it, who you are and your identity morphs into something independent of what you look like or who you are to others. It is of no reassurance that the senses I had before were imperfect and unrefined. If I was once the humans that inhabited the earth, then it stands to reason that what I sense is all a fiction I created using the tools given to us through the process of evolution so that we could survive through the many dangers that faced us within our past. However, the dangers that I face, if they can be called that, are of a different nature now, and evolution despite its effectiveness has only provided me with crude tools that allowed for us to survive and do nothing else.

I feel as though I am a part of the empty space around me, melting into the void, as though I am the darkness which has become sentient. I do not know if this is real or this is a simulation, but there has to be something I can do. I refuse to believe that I have absolutely no control over my fate, that I am only living a life that has been predetermined by some laws governing reality that I do not comprehend. I have no limbs to call my own, but occasionally, I imagine sensations of the hands that should be there, like phantom limbs after an amputation. Am I truly helpless, fated to be a slave to the cosmos, watching it wither? That cannot be. I cannot see my arms, hands, or thumbs, but this form may not be completely worthless. What if it is a matter of understanding this form to become a master of our destiny? When I lost my legs and arms in the past, when I lost my body, I created prosthetics and learned to control those over time. I do not know what means I have to control my environment, but if I needed to walk and I did not know if I had legs, then I would have never walked.

"This is illogical, we have no proof."

I am unaware of the options that are laid out before me, but if they are there, then all it takes is a little bit of patience. The only way we still have a chance of imposing our will on the universe is by using my imagination and trying to move all the phantom limbs I may or may not have. It will be a long journey. I might not ever find the right muscle to flex, or comprehend the right approach to mastering this form, but I have all the time in the universe. As illogical as it may be, there has always been room for another religion. Let's see what we can do.

PART 2

Escape from the Real

CHAPTER 7: THE DEGENERATE ERA

We now stand witness to the beginnings of the Degenerate Era. The birth of new celestial bodies have been replaced by an aging population of stars, black holes, and crumbling solar systems, marking a time of decay. It is the end result of the passage of quadrillions of Earth years. The best of our lives are now behind us. This is the beginning of old age— of decline. The beginnings of a death march can be seen here leaving behind a deep, dark trail of blood. The stars that still exist are white dwarfs, brown dwarfs, neutron stars, or have collapsed into a black hole. The vibrant nebulae that spanned light years and painted the darkness in bright hues have been consumed to form their own collections of stellar bodies and are now nothing more than husks of their former selves. In this dying universe, life still exists, but struggles to carry on in traditional forms. There are alternate forms of life that operate using entire expanses of empty space as a way to maintain some form of genetic data. Like a tree is to a human, these alternate lifeforms operate on time scales that are incomprehensible to the traditional forms we saw in the past. Traditional forms of life cling to any remaining planets and stars like shipwreck survivors drifting at sea. They exist either in the form of highly advanced civilizations capable of using their technological prowess to combat the aging nature of the universe, or in the form of extremophiles which are capable of surviving in extreme conditions in a rudimentary manner. Even in this hopeless situation, life can adapt to reach sufficient levels of resilience against the pressures of their environment when such shifting pressures do not change too quickly. "Too quickly", is of little concern in this era, however.

The lengthening of time scales and the increasing rate of expansion of the universe indicate an asymptote in terms of how complexity manifests. For many civilizations that are merely surviving, the resources needed to migrate to a star system or another galaxy simply do not exist anymore or are decreasing. It is as though there is drought approaching the oases in the desert, and what good soil remains is quickly turning to dry sand.

The resources needed for large-scale projects that can potentially create new discoveries needed to break off the current cycles of meager subsistence are insufficient. Civilizations that have escaped an existence akin to vagrants gathered around a fire in a blizzard have found a way to survive. They have either escaped their fate or become self-sufficient to the point where the fate of the universe no longer concerns them by collecting the necessary materials in time.

Civilizations that have long since freed themselves from the fate shared by those in this era have escaped this universe to start a life elsewhere by mastering other dimensions or realities to bend to their will appropriately. Others have simply traveled to the past to enjoy a time that was far more pleasant without needing to worry about alternative laws of physics and only concerned themselves with the equally complex problem of time paradoxes. For those that have become self-sufficient, they have transformed themselves into creatures no longer requiring high levels of energy to sustain life while creating artificial environments capable of traveling the vastness of space for indefinite periods of time using alternate forms of matter. These groups of intelligent life have seen the writing on the wall and hoarded physical matter and heat precisely to lengthen the lifespan of their species. This is the dichotomy of traditional intelligent life: either fleeing the dangers of the cosmos or fighting to the death against the elements in the hope that each additional second is worth it, no matter how painful or costly.

In the journey towards the end of the universe, Humanity changed from an entity that stagnantly floated within a single solar system to an entity that managed to travel vast distances over a cosmic timescale. What started as miniscule acceleration unnoticeable to a human added up over trillions of years to become interplanetary, interstellar, and eventually intergalactic travel. Like the moving of tectonic plates, incremental changes lead to massive results. The being sped up as though with each attempt to move its phantom limbs moved it faster and faster along its adventure through the universe. A trip that started near Earth then guided it past the orbit of Jupiter, through the Oort cloud and the empty regions between Sol and Proxima Centauri which was the next closest star. It rushed past Proxima Centauri and then moved through many other solar systems at rapid speed over billions of years. Among its determined path were a variety of sights. From red giants to nebulae, to a journey through a black hole unaffected by gravity, Humanity was given a full course of sights which it may have never seen if it was never cursed into its form— a form which has shown slight changes over the course of its exploration of creation.

Lines began to form, like divisions, splitting the ball of ephemeral flesh into sections like a developing morula consisting of a rapidly developing set of cells originating from a fertilized egg cell. These ridges were deep like uniform canyons that spanned the entirety of the planetoid. They were perfect, as though they were engineered instead of the product of natural processes. Despite these dramatic changes, nothing was felt, and nothing was noticed. The development of this creature, and to what end, was only observed by those who chose to follow and observe it in its race through the cosmos.

These followers gathered early during the Stelliferous era, fervently matched pace with Humanity throughout the years. The followers studied its existence, but all were unable to determine what Humanity was, fueling an obsession to find the truth. Over the course of the trillions of years, the races that followed transformed from biological forms to those that were hybrids, utilizing the power of machines in combination with the optimizations brought upon by evolution and genetic engineering to create populations that were truly capable of space-faring. Wherever Humanity went, was a remnant in the form of colonies as these civilizations left traces of themselves like a trail of breadcrumbs. As these civilizations advanced, they engineered entire solar systems into unique machines and forms spanning entire astronomical units for the enabling of their pursuit. They followed Humanity as though it was a guiding beacon of light to lead them through the vastness of creation, splintering and rejoining millennia later as the result of ideological division. For some, the Entity was the answers to all their questions. For others who disagreed, Humanity was simply a natural phenomenon beyond their understanding and an unnecessary danger that brought no immediate profit for those who tirelessly pursued the planetoid across solar systems. These disagreements resulted in interplanetary wars which sought to monopolize resources for one cause or the other with each faction prioritizing different resources, resulting in a fracturing of the populations. However, these interplanetary wars were of no concern to the planetoid cruising along its predetermined path, and soon, the followers abandoned their conflicts over the colonies to steadfastly continue their observance of the entity leaving those with no interest behind to colonize the regions of space that were previously fought over.

This buzz of activity around the galactic quadrant which Humanity occupied eventually drew other followers who flocked to the ethereal sphere in hopes that it could fulfill their wishes. From a yearning for riches, to answers to scientific questions, to a desire to understand the divine, each visitor had its own designs for the anomaly. This led to millions of years of interstellar wars which forced some civilizations out of the running while others adapted quickly, co-opting and reverse engineering the technologies of their enemies to suit their needs. Through either progression or assimilation, the different civilizations gradually found themselves reaching a stalemate as well as an understanding. Those who ended these conflicts to monopolize the space around the entity realized that they were not the same as the ones who started them an eon ago. These civilizations changed over the millennia. Some democracies became monarchies. Some theocracies became technocracies ruled by AI while continuing to worship Humanity as a symbol resembling objects which seeded all of creation as though it was the physical manifestation of myths and religions that were incepted at a time when these societies were still only capable of producing bronze tools. The reasons for conflict no longer applied. And as all who followed the path of Humanity realized that their time and resources would run out, they banded together, some choosing to stay behind, while others chose to follow, merging into a series of collectives that cooperated and communicated despite cultural, physical, and cosmic boundaries. Empires rose and fell, but the heat death of the universe was inevitable, which meant that conflict given a finite period of time was counterproductive.

With the passage of time came the ebb and flow of new visitors and the departures of old companions. Some who worshiped the entity as a divine figure followed dogmatically even as it reached near the speed of light. Others dropped away, unable to sustain their chase across the stars, vanishing from humanity's sight and into the shadows. And then there were those who were faced with a choice. To stay in this universe or leave to another time or reality. These patterns and events continued, on and on, over the trillions of years, eventually leaving the barren planetoid in the same position it was in when it started: alone and staring into the darkness.

However, the darkness here was far grimmer. The stars that dotted the blackness were vanishing, stealing away any companions that could save humanity from solitude with them. Yes, there is a chance for reunions. However, in this expanding universe that grows dimmer and dimmer, as time passes, that chance approaches zero like a countdown clock ticking down towards the death of creation.

CHAPTER 8: THE MIRACULOUS ODYSSEY TOWARDS ADVERSITY

The memories of my early childhood are few and obscure. It is all a blur regardless of the life I lived, as though I've simply dreamed those moments. Things such as socio-economic conditions, the words spoken around me, where I've been, and where I planned to go were the first things I forgot. I was once a completely different person. However, who that person was is shrouded in the fog of time. What does stand out among the muddled past that is childhood are the senses and emotions— what I felt, when I felt them. The smell was also strangely vivid despite not knowing what it was. Was it plastic, or some kind of chemical in the common household like a fabric softener? Context is absent, and worries non-existent. I lived only in the present, unable to think back upon a past, and unwilling to ponder the future. Direction was a strange concept. I could move myself left, right, up, down, forward, and backwards, but not understand or comprehend a final destination in the initial stages. I thought not of where I should go, but simply what I wanted to do, and eventually I would arrive at my destination through a series of misguided actions where I crawled along to wherever I wanted to be without caring where I was, or what dangers were strewn along my path. It was instinct over wisdom. Feeling over experience. Present pain took any priority over future pain, and the absence of pain in the present meant the absence of pain in the future. There was only me, and what others could offer me. Cause and effect, action and consequence. None of this meant anything for me. I simply wanted. I simply did. And in the process, I simply learned. Which brought me to the decision to take my first step.

I am not sure what brought me up from the ground in all those lives. Was it madness, or a wish for greater freedom? Maybe it was the strings of fate lifting me up from the ground, pushing me in the direction of whatever I was meant to be. Maybe seeing those who cared for me walk unhampered made me realize my limitations. This clumsy body was clearly not enough for me despite it acting as a governor on my stupidity. I crawled along, sometimes on hard floor, sometimes on carpet, sometimes not even underneath a roof, but I crawled towards anything I could use to support myself. I would balance myself as I moved my body up the vertical support so that I could place my torso above my legs. This step alone was quite challenging, as I would often either slip and fall forward, or push myself up too hard, lose balance, and fall backwards. It was only through the process of repetition that I was able to place myself upright on two legs long enough that I had the leisure to look around at my accomplishments as though I were the ruler of a kingdom. Feeling ambitious, I might try to move onto the next step and put one foot forward only to fall flat on my face and then wail in response to this great injustice. Of course, this too would pass, and even the need for a vertical support would be unnecessary.

Often, my efforts would be independent, but when they were noticed, I would receive help in some form or other. Those who cared for me would raise me up, catch me before I fall, and wait some distance away so as to encourage me towards a destination that was leagues away. I did not understand what they were saying, but what I could make out in the tone of speech, the facial expressions, and the body language, only convinced me that I was on the right track. I did not understand what a parent even was. I did not have a clear understanding on what our connection was, how we were related, or why I was being cared for despite expecting a certain level of care. In spite of this, I could feel something drawing us together. Perhaps to our parents, we were merely a burden. However, at the time, I felt a feeling of safety, of comfort. I did not know or care to know of what I was being protected from, but I held the greatest confidence in the abilities of someone who I only knew for a short period of time. The moment I saw them, they had my trust even though I had no one else I could trust. There was a feeling of attachment I could not quite explain. If there was a place I could call home, it was because they were there, waiting for me. There was an emotional bond, built over a short period of time, a bond that had no backing. It was strong, and it was unconditional. Still, to this day, I do not know why I could foolishly conclude that those feelings of security, assurance, relief, and erratic joy which came and went were real, but my obstinate belief in my feelings rather than reality often led to those feelings becoming reality. That could be what it means to be family.

While I did not realize it at the time, the impressive nature of what I did in those many instances does not escape me now. I used an undeveloped body with weak legs and stubby toes to walk. I know how difficult that is for animals, for robots, and even some people. Despite this, I succeeded billions of times while using tools that were only barely up to the task, like chopping wood with a dull ax, or starting a fire with merely twigs and rocks. It is possible, but it was laborious.

Each day, with each time, I would add another step to my personal record. I would make it further and further, and my body would change and adapt to help me. Then, one day, I reached the end, and what was once one of the greatest challenges simply became a milestone on a series of landmarks along the way to old age and eventually death. From that moment, my greatest concerns would continue to be forward looking, while occasionally being grateful for the past. I rarely considered the series of events that led up to this point, and took whatever occurred for granted irrespective of how improbable as though I deserved it and was entitled to it for simply being alive. Every time I looked back, all I thought was how quickly time passed as though everything was a whirl when in reality, the passage of time did not quicken nor slow. I did not worry about the probabilities involved in the formation of our star. I did not care about all that lived before us and the well tread path that was given to us. I did not consider the unlikeliness of my existence.

To reach this point, an infinite series of events needed to occur. The universe needed to form, and our reality needed to have certain rules. Time needed to flow forward. Matter needed to exist. The Earth needed to be placed in the appropriate location within the solar system. It needed a moon and the gravitational force it exerted. It needed the right combination of elements and molecules and a certain amount of energy for the formation of the foundational building blocks of life. Life itself had certain requirements. It needed to be able to generate energy and grow over time, eventually reproducing. It needed a safe environment that did not change too often so that it was not wiped out completely. And that was the bare minimum before it could grow into more complex forms.

The features of humans that were seen when I was still on Earth: multicellular structures, organs, vertebrae, limbs, sensory organs, a brain capable of complex behavior took billions of years and required many extinction events to allow for their development. We, the descendants of those who cowered before the apex predators of past eras only came into being because we had our chance to stand in the sun and grow unimpeded into the upright form associated with humans. It was luck, and little intention that brought us to this point. Evidently, the many factors that played a role were billions of years in the making and beyond our control.

Even when considering events after the appearance of Homo Sapiens, there was no shortage of things that had to go right to bring us to this point. Ignoring all the inventions, the rise and fall of civilizations, when looking at what individuals themselves needed to accomplish, it is quite clear that all of the stars needed to align accordingly. Our ancestors needed to survive genocides, disasters, and outlive their competition long enough to form families and find offspring. What of my parents —these people who stood at the end of a room waiting for me to walk towards them with the utmost patience?

My parents needed to be born, and they needed to be born without severe defects or impairments. They needed to live long enough to reach the point where they could meet, know one another, and decide to stay together. They had to be in a position of relative stability, both in terms of maturity and finances to allow for the support of their future child. This typically meant being able to maintain a profession, having the educational credentials to gain that position, and the right type of upbringing needed to succeed within an imperfect educational system. Then, there is the task of conception, a stage where much could go wrong. The joining of gametes, a sperm and an egg cell, to fertilize into a zygote is one of a game of extreme probability and competition. Where one sperm cell ultimately fertilizes an egg, millions fail, and in the process the gender, and many of the genetic qualities of the offspring are decided. Two sets of twenty-three chromosomes join to become forty-six, forming a full genetic picture of who this child may become if all goes according to plan. What follows is the development of an embryo over the course of nine months as it divides and grows into a fetus. One often wonders when this collection of cells becomes a human, but what is quite clear is that there is a point where this alien soul turns from something subjectively perceived as merely a clump of flesh to something that might be more, something that is human. Where this point lies is unclear, and dependent on each person. To some, the child does not feel human even after birth, and it is only when it is able to express itself meaningfully that it is acknowledged as a human with intelligent thoughts and self-awareness. While for others, the human spark started well before its conception, as though the human was born billions of years before it even gained a physical form. There is no denying that the connection between the mother and the child leads to the question of whether these were two individuals prior to birth instead of just one.

How connected are we, and are we more the same than we are different? We were all borne from the same processes, perhaps fated to exist from the moment the universe was incepted. Maybe we are simply many expressions of the same thing, and not truly all that different. Maybe we are not multiple individuals, but simply one being with multiple souls. Maybe the series of dominoes that led to this moment would always fall in the same way, leading to what I have become now. If we hate one another, then do I hate myself? When we were at odds with one another, was I simply thinking myself into a corner rather than working to solve the problems at hand? Though I was given this chance, to exist despite all the challenges, maybe I squandered my chance, and continue to squander my chance simply due to my nature.

The notion that I have nothing but squandered chances lying in store for me is a fear I have that dwarfs all other fears, and I am terrified that I can do nothing about it. Whenever I am reminded of this, all the joyful moments of the past morph into demons that torment me with prophecies of rapture and judgment in the future. To this day, I still do not know who I am, and what I want to be. I can barely remember the children I once were. In place of the childlike wonder I had and the liberty I felt despite being only a child, is a deafening cynicism that stands in stark contrast to what we once were. Whether this is cause to be afraid is something I have yet to know and yet I still dread whatever is to come next despite knowing nothing. The boundless nature of simply being is no longer. We have cherished it, and we have forgotten it.

CHAPTER 9: INFINITE FAILURE

The sights I've seen have left an indelible impression on me that may last to the end of the universe. It is almost as though I could be misled into thinking the wait was worth it. We once believed that to see what, in the past, could only be viewed from far away with a telescope up close would be an impossibility that I would never experience within my lifetime. However, I have been given the privilege of exactly that, and for that I am grateful. In exchange, we were required to temper our patience to a level we have not reached before. A level that is orders of magnitude beyond any meditation, any prison sentence, and any ordeal. The human mind was not designed for such a thing, and yet here we are. It is a mental marathon of unprecedented proportions. It seems that our plight was predetermined and any struggles were ultimately futile. In such a situation, patience and resilience were the closest thing to stopgaps which could save us from the periodic episodes of plunging into mental abysses from which we escaped only by clawing our way out. It was a meager existence of falling in and climbing desperately out over and over again with no end in sight. To expect anything was a worthless enterprise.

Initially, there was hope, or at least more of it than there is now. Jupiter, the ruler of this outer realm, shined with a brilliant light and is adorned with spots that glow like embers in the night sky. Its gaseous exterior, a tapestry of golds, oranges and reds, created a visage of grandeur and splendor that acted as a lantern in our lonely travels. Past the orbit of Jupiter, we watched ourselves fly off into space, with increasing speeds over the centuries and millennia. Time was something we had no shortage of, but the smallest of pains and most miniscule of ordeals could lengthen time like a black hole tearing apart matter and stretching it into unimaginably long segments. The time I spent to reach where I am now has been long, but it felt longer, and eventually, it lost the meaning that it once held to a being with a mortal's perspective. In a life with seemingly infinite time, there is no such thing as incorrect actions, imperfections or failures. Anything that is wrong can be corrected. With that said, when you are incapable of doing anything, you cannot make a mistake even if you tried. Similarly, if you did something wrong, you are unable to correct it. In the place of action is an emptiness that emanates from this existence to watch time flow as you are unable to do act. Free will as I knew it was a thing of the past. I could not impose my will upon the universe or reality. Almost everything was as though it is set in stone. Everything, but the universe around me. It still endured.

The universe I saw was beautiful. That much was undeniable. However, it was unbearably cold and unfeeling. When you look into the lights off in the distance, you can use your imagination, but it is anyone's guess as to whether someone is looking back. As I accelerated and left the domain of planets and entered the realm of comets and interstellar space, I found myself missing the large companions that were among the closest things I could call friends in this island of matter floating in an ocean of empty space. It is undeniable that the more mass there is accumulated, the more chances there are for something interesting to happen. It is hard to create storms on an asteroid, or life on a small rock. You need size for that, and a lot of it. The smaller bodies have no moons, no core, no magnetic fields, and are basically fodder for the larger planets, or orphaned in space where nothing can touch it. Out there, in the space between systems, the pull of gravity is weak, and if you were stranded out there with no fuel, all you can do is simply wait and hope that you can be saved as your distance from any nearby stars implies that you won't be lucky enough to be within the gravitational pull of any system. I, however, am no astronaut, cosmonaut, or taikonaut in need of life support. There is no one here to save me.

The empty region between these systems is where I spent billions of years, waiting for whatever it was that propelled me to send me along my way to a place that was not simply black. It was once I reached Proxima Centauri that I realized how quickly I was traveling. Although it was not even remotely close to the speeds reached by the Voyager probes, it was fast enough to ensure I did not overstay my welcome. I was only within the system for hundreds of millions of years. I understood then that my destiny was one of multiple systems, and of many sights. While reassuring, this fact led to poisonous anticipation. I zipped past the planets of Proxima Centauri, appreciating its similarities to and its differences from our own sun. Proxima Centauri, unlike our own sun, was significantly smaller as it was a red dwarf. In our time, it was a faint star that was dismissed as being capable of holding life. Whether that dismissal was fair or not is questionable, but it is true that even the faintest of stars can be incredibly luminous up close. A large ball of fire is still a large ball of fire and its intensity was befitting of its pedigree. A star is still a star no matter how small. It was here that I noticed that I had a follower. The descendants of whomever sent the first probe had sent another one which matched pace with my predetermined path. Its droplet-like form glistened when it caught the light at the right angle and made for a welcome presence in an otherwise desolate scene. I wondered then whether the makers of this machine lived nearby— perhaps in one of the planets I had passed. What about the planets orbiting my sun? Now that I am gone, who is it that calls it home?

Perhaps someone more responsible is in charge now. Maybe my follower occupied the planet and terraformed it for their needs. Conversely, one of the other residents of Earth may be filling our shoes. I wonder which species it might be. The dolphins were limited to the oceans. The elephants are quite intelligent, but would they be able to match what we did in our prime? The chimpanzees and bonobos have a chance. When we still had hands, we could communicate using sign language and pass on knowledge in a somewhat limited capacity. Oh how I wish we could see what happened, what unique forms of life could flower in our absence. I could only grab a glimpse of this probe when it was in front of me, and when I did, I was unable to understand its form. How was it manufactured? What is it made of? How is it traveling? I was so curious. Here, in front of me was a probe far more advanced than anything humanity had ever built. It was smooth, beautiful, and unmarred as though it was more a striking work of art instead of a spacefaring vessel. The materials and the methods by which it moved were beyond our intellect. It was proof of a civilization that managed to live long enough to avoid the mistakes we made. What did the people who made this look like? Were they like us with symmetry, with a vertebrae, two legs, and hands with opposable thumbs? Or were they completely alien, taking on a form that we could not even imagine? Perhaps they were not even carbon based or used DNA as a form of genetic storage. Maybe they were no longer biological. I hoped we have similar values, and a similar sense of wonder towards everything. I hoped that if we could communicate that we would be able to find common ground and understand one another. If intelligence is accompanied by curiosity and a balancing of exploration and exploitation of the environment, then maybe we are more similar than we think. Indeed, the cosmos is too barren for what little life that sprouts to regard everything with suspicion all the time.

These past musings only served to keep me entertained, but I was ultimately unable to answer a single question. Once I passed Proxima Centauri, my path approached several systems, but ultimately never entered their orbit, and I could only watch as these systems swung by on my flight towards a nebula. The swirling clouds of gas and dust that made up these nebulae, danced and played in a cosmic ballet, creating patterns and shapes that seemed to defy imagination. Their vibrant hues, ranging from deep blues and purples to fiery oranges and reds, painted a canvas of color that was both mesmerizing and awe-inspiring. From a distance, this bright cloud of gas and particulate matter was an imposing structure which colored the tapestry of the galaxy felt as though it was a solid body that held as much activity as an asteroid field, but upon my entering this cloud, I could clearly understand that it was more impressive from afar than it was within. The gas and matter that colored the nebula was extremely diffuse which meant that like all things in the universe, the majority of it was composed of empty space. There is so much all around us, but when viewed in close proximity, it just looks like empty black. It was when I reached budding stars and planets which grew from the dust that I could truly savor and appreciate the existence of these clouds of matter. It was here that I could see the formation of solar systems much like my own right before me. These balls of dust could one day be home to life of its own which grows to reach for the stars much like my companion has and I did in the far past. As I passed through the clouds and continued on my way, I watched on, hopeful and almost envious of the opportunity that lay ahead for the life that would inhabit these systems.

By this point, my speed was an order of magnitude higher, and my visits to systems increased tenfold, granting me the opportunity to see many more unique sights at higher frequency. All while gaining more followers. I ran the gamut of the cycle of life for stars. There were stars of differing colors from those which matched the white of our sun to others which were older and grew to red giants, swallowing its closest planet. I was in the center of a dead system when a white dwarf rained fire across space in the form of a supernova. Finally, I had the chance to see my first black hole. Rather, I did not necessarily see it, but I saw its effects. I observed how it used its gravitational heft to swallow all matter that unwittingly entered its pull. I saw how it bent and warped light to show us hints of what lay on its periphery. It made no sound, but I imagine if it could, it would have had a deafening roar that tore across the galaxy unheard by none. As I passed through the gravitational pull of the black hole unimpeded, my follower needed to take the long way around to meet me on the other side. The sight of light warping into strange geometries as I approached the center was bizarre, and it led me to question all the theories that were formulated in the past. While I could simply pass through, my followers had to utilize the black hole to slingshot themselves in my general direction so that it was able to keep up, and in the process, most likely experienced untold amounts of time dilation. I do not know what the lifespan of the creatures that built these spacefaring objects are, but what is clear is that they have either exceeded and surpassed biological limits, or that such limits no longer apply. If they could keep pace with me for millions and billions of years, then it stands to reason that the probes were not carrying biological life. If so, what does that imply for the civilizations that built them? Were these machines simply carrying out instructions given to them without end while their masters crumbled away into dust due to the passage of time? Or have the makers of these machines transcended life and death? I hope that the friends I have yet to meet are not already gone.

In the end, I inwardly decided to move on, and these questions faded away as I continued to accelerate. I was hoping I could catch my former solar system if it had not turned into a shell of its former self through some disaster or as the result of simple aging. This was not to be, however. Reality was unfortunately not merciful, and we missed it by tens of thousands of light years. Our last chance of seeing our former home was ripped away by the cruel touch of reality which decided that the path we must take was in a different direction. Instead, we continued our tour of the galaxy, passing much of what it had to offer to arrive at a ternary collection of black holes slowly revolving around one another in a ballet of destruction, turning all within its surroundings into emaciated ghosts. Light played in this configuration like a demented prism, not simply being warped, but also mirrored in some cases. In a moment of what I believe to be the benevolence of fate, I was in the right position at the right time as a star passed by my position, lighting my body in visible light, and granting me a muddied look at what I had become. Off in the distance, as though there was a copy of me out there, I could see an image of myself and my followers contorted by the effects of gravity.

A large mass, uneven and bizarre floated across the sky with shining metal behind it like a piper leading mice. It held the consistency of discolored meat, with uneven growths all across it. Like something mutated by radiation, it was inconsistent, and yet it had a familiar geometry like a polyhedron formed of multiple spheres. I could not place where I last saw a similar thing. Was it fungus? Perhaps a plant of some kind. Regardless, it felt alive, and that was what was most terrifying. That something so large could have a mind of its own and intrude upon any corner of the universe unimpeded. It moved consistently— more like a robot with a set of preprogrammed actions than a creature with a set of emotions and motivations. There was no sense of exploration, curiosity, or discovery in its movements. It was simply a large mass of flesh following a path as though wherever it needed to go, it needed to reach it quickly and efficiently. This scene was the first and last moment I would see of myself. Any changes and developments, good and horrifying, would go on to be unobserved by us in our future wanderings towards the end of time.

That was when I began to lose track of time. I would count inside my head, keeping track of the seconds, or at least trying to achieve a close estimate. At some point, I simply gave up, and the increasing speed was of no help either. Although my perception of time may explain how much time passed for me, it does not tell us how much time has passed in the greater universe. I left the Milky Way galaxy with my companions in tow and left for the realm of nomads, strangers, and orphans, where everything was an endangered species. Here, there was even less than there was in the emptiness of the galaxy. The spaces grew wider, and I began to approach speeds that resulted in time dilation. I felt as though I was chasing after cars and watching them fly away. Whatever light there was formed streaks in my vision, blurring my periphery while the galaxies off in the distance shone brightly in a seductive manner. They were beckoning to me to visit. I realized, however, that the chances of sojourning to such large places were slim. As far away as planets and stars were from one another, that did not even remotely compare with that of galaxies. Even the Andromeda galaxy, which was our closest neighbor, was millions of light years away, and at this point, I understood that the world of matter and light was in the minority, and nothingness was to be my reality for the foreseeable future. Even with the dilation of time, it is still a long period of time to witness the dying of creation.

It was just like that stage in life where I was behind bars in a cell. Time passed, but I could no longer tell. The outside world to me was just bland concrete and unchanging routine forced onto all of us at the prison. The meals were the same, the smell was the same, and nothing changed. But I knew and everyone else knew that the world was changing. It was changing without us, running on its own schedule, moving on without us. We were no longer needed. We no longer mattered. The tick tock of the world would not stop just because I was not there to witness it myself. My family moved on. They had no choice but to move on, and I needed to resign myself to this fact. My needs were nothing, and it was only selfish for my situation to hold back the lives of those I loved. It must have been the same for everyone else. I know it was the same for so many of my lives that spent significant portions of their time incarcerated. God has left the building, and did not take me upon his exit.

The unreasonable nature of the situation did not matter. Whether I spent my time inside an empty apartment, a jail cell, or strapped to a hospital bed, no one cared who I was. No one cared if I lived or died. I was just one in billions, a drop in a sea of people. It does not matter what I think, the rest of reality moves on. It did not revolve around us back then, and it did not do so now. The center of the universe is elsewhere. It is anywhere except where I am. Here in this cell, there is only me. There is not much space to move, but there is much time to think as I stretch my limbs every time they start to cramp.

Regardless of where I was, where I am, when I lived, and who I am, the only thing I was entitled to were my own thoughts, and now, those were the most valuable possessions I had. The universe may forget us, but we refuse to forget ourselves and lose ourselves within the void.

CHAPTER 10: THE LIVES OF OTHERS

My childhood was a missed opportunity, but there is no reason why I cannot have another one, or many others. There were many instances where I looked at my present self and wondered when I had become an adult despite not maturing in any way. It seems as though the only difference between a child and an adult is years spent alive and physical differences. The rest was determined by society. But here, there is no society. We can be whatever we wish and rewrite the rules as we see fit.

Yes, here I am, there is a playground. What should I include in it? A slide, some swings, a few trees and rocks to climb, and unlimited recess. Sounds great. But there's something missing. Oh yes. Friends. How many should I have? I should have a lot. But that sounds tiresome. Maybe just the right amount. Yes. Just a few. Just the ones that matter. Everyone else can be a backdrop. Want to play with me? No, you seem icky. Want to play tag? Great. You can be it. Everyone gets caught except me. The playground isn't enough. There's the forest right there. What, the teachers will stop us? Fine. No more teachers then. Or, how about a change of plans? Picnic in the woods. The whole class is invited. You can carry the picnic basket and I'll hold onto the picnic blanket. The colors are red and white of course. What are we having to eat? Some sandwiches? How traditional, but just right. A picnic basket is like a magic box! It's so big and has a handle so you can carry it. Inside, there's all sorts of yummy treats like sandwiches and fruit and cookies! You just can't beat the classics. I don't know why we did not do things like this more often. I did not learn anything in school anyways, and sniffing glue all day gets boring after a while. Let's go deeper. We have to be back in time? No we don't. Recess is forever. The fun will never end. We can forget all about homework, math, and those awful school lunches. We can be here as long as we want. There is nothing to drag us back, and there is no reason to go back. This is it. A scene of peace and serene calm. What? There is a monster? We can just slay it, like those heroes in our favorite books. Nothing can stop us. Anything is possible. This is what I missed. It's everything I wanted that I never had a chance to enjoy.

"Enough of this. I want to experience something else."

Today is a busy day like all others. I enter the campus, swipe my card, and make my way to my cubicle which has my name plate on it. The lighting is the same as it is every day. It is bright enough to read text, but dark enough to give you a headache by the end of the day. The room temperature is set to a sub 70 degree Fahrenheit level. I boot my computer up. So, what do I have on the schedule today? Yes, today we're finishing up our product and launching. The scene was electric as our leadership eagerly awaited the unveiling of the latest offering. It is not just a matter of sending out a finished product on time, but polishing it so that it is a good product rather than a mediocre one that can easily be overtaken by any competitors and upstarts. After all, first impressions are key. We need to iron out the bugs, test it multiple times, and ensure that no stone is left unturned. I take the lead, guiding and mentoring younger workers on their tasks so that we can hit the deadline without any problems. Although it takes us well into the evening, we make good progress. With careful planning and a systematic approach, we finish the day with a successful launch and good reviews. A job well done.

"You could dream up anything and this is what you chose to think about?"

I walk into work the next day with a sense of purpose.

I swipe my employee badge and stroll past security back to my desk. I set my pc up and start looking at what our tasks are for the day. I am called into a meeting with my manager and am showered with compliments. It turns out that the product launch is leading to numbers and figures that indicate a promising trend in gaining market share. Software tends to be like that. If you have a good product that gives people what they want that is lacking in the competition, you can even any gaps without necessarily needing to have many resources or even people. I do not know how much profit my actions would ultimately lead to, but what was clear was I believed in the mission. We are making the world a better place, and I am playing a large role in the journey to a better world. I matter.

"It's too mundane."

The temple in which I reside is usually quite peaceful and somewhat remote. The duties of a monk, while demanding a living that is lacking in modern luxuries is rewarding once appreciated. The daily routine of tending to the temple grounds can be monotonous, but the four seasons give the chores a bit of variety throughout the year. The temple, while being a place of meditation and worship, is also a reflection of my work. Whether it is clean, whether it is ruined or well-maintained is all a result of my labor. There is always something falling apart in this aging temple, so the fine treatment witnessed here is, in some sense, proof of a lifetime of devotion and care. There is a certain level of pride in seeing the outcome of hardship that makes it seem as though it is all worth it even when knowing and understanding that the temple will still wither away over time. When I pass, when no one is around to keep this collection of stone in one piece, it will become dust. However, I still continue. I clean the grounds, I care for the fish in the ponds and till the stones in the garden. I continue to recite mantras and write sutras. I enjoy the peace, and I find comfort in the hardship. Suffering is a fundamental aspect of the human experience. Pain and death is as well. To be deprived of these things would mean an inhuman and lacking life. I welcome the moment, good and bad. It is all a part of a full experience.

If I were at peace, maybe I could feel the same about this moment as well. In many ways, I wish for pain, suffering, and death. I wish to be human, to experience human things, to have a fear of the future or fear for a future I care about and realize the fear is merely a creation of our own making. However, the parts of me that are at peace are merely a small minority in a mob of unsatisfied and confused individuals. If I had a chance, some way to frame this as necessary and in a positive manner, perhaps we can convince the others to live in the moment. The moment is what matters, and that one should enjoy it while it lasts and not take it for granted. You do not know what the future brings, but change is inevitable. I tell the rest of myself this. Some parts of me listen. Some do not. Some progress is made, but soon, everything returns back to its original state. We want to live in the moment, but to many, this moment is a never ending disappointment that we are unwilling to accept.

CHAPTER 11: WHY

The loop of loathing formed by my thoughts always touches upon the same question over and over like Chinese water torture breaking my spirit. It won't kill you, unfortunately, but will drive you mad. Am I mad? I no longer know. What determines whether I am sane or not is what the average person thinks. But I am as average as they come. There is only me. So, am I sane, or am I mad? It does not matter. I cannot harm anyone or lead anyone down our path of insanity. All we can do is think our thoughts and eventually ask, "Why? Why?" as I always have.

So what was it that I did wrong? What sins did I commit to deserve this? Why me? Indeed, they are too numerous to count. There is not an innocent soul among us. We are born a mistake, an imperfection that will always fall into sin. This is what it means to be human. However, within the midst of desires and failings, there are moments, missions where we are allowed to redeem ourselves. The form this takes is different for each person, but to say that the fruit of human labor is from a barren field is disingenuous in the least. But was it enough? Was it enough to justify our existence? Arguably, we did not advocate our worth through our actions. Perhaps our worth as human beings was insufficient to allow us to savor the privilege of our mortal lives.

"It depends on what defines our value," an economist cut in. "In an economy, our wealth is defined by a number of variables from our income which is based on the value of our labor to our assets which can grow in value over time. These things have a value that is decided by a market. When it comes to our current situation, economics may not apply. Supply and demand is vague. We want something and there is no supply. In addition to this, there is nothing we can provide in exchange. At least nothing that we are aware of. Whatever our situation is, it is currently not defined by a market where there is a buyer and a seller."

Whatever it was that we once stood for was vague and became perverted to suit our needs. Certainly, it could be said that we as a people have morphed into fiends that the principles that we found oh so sacred and cherished. The ugliness of humanity has been on full display for the majority of our existence, but in the few centuries before we took this form, it has reached a scale that was unprecedented. Suffering was an industry. Damage was an industry. We became good at it and optimized it as though it was an essential part a manufacturing pipeline. We turned it into a mantra, an anthem, and made it the new set of commandments supporting the new world order.

Cheapen the labor. Slash and burn. Push them out into the cold streets. Leave them to die. Place them in chains. Poison the well after drinking from it. Take their souls. Own their bodies. Take their wealth. Leave them with nothing. Have them beg for a morsel. Make them grateful for what little they have. Distract them from the truth. Take what's mine. Pillage. Plunder. Celebrate it all as achievements. Eat when you are hungry. Drink when you are thirsty. Don't ask for permission. If it's not legal, make it legal. If it is not law, pay to make it so. If you don't have the cash, take it from those who do. The world is your oyster. Once you have your pearl, nothing else matters. Meet your deadlines. Take your shortcuts. It doesn't matter if you are right or wrong. What matters is if you get there. Move fast and break things. Break them beyond repair if you need to. What is better is what I decide. What is good is what I decide. Only keep up appearances as long as you need to. Loyalty is merely a tool. Everyone is just a stepping stone. Win no matter the cost. Second place is just the first loser. Sympathy is for fools. Can't pay? Get lost. Can't work? Good riddance. Is that public property? Not anymore it isn't. You're not good enough. You're not hungry enough. You're not strong enough. You're not smart enough. Oh you need that to live? Then I guess that's all your life is worth. I write the agenda. I tell the story. You are just a side character. I matter. You don't. I'm right. You're wrong. You're worthless. I'm priceless. I can find more of you even if I didn't try. You are a number. You are a dollar sign. What's yours is mine, and what's mine is mine. You made this? No, I did.

"We have always arranged ourselves into a hierarchy," someone said. "For someone to stand at the top, others must be at the bottom. As humans, we spend our time comparing ourselves to one another to understand our level of success and failure. If everyone was the same, then everyone is average. Everyone is unremarkable. That means that there is nothing to distinguish you from anyone else. We all become equally special and equally worthless."

Be it through pride, stupidity, shame, greed, guilt, envy or a mixture of these qualities, the ugliness of humanity is clear to see when it is on full display. In the past when information was limited to the privileged, it was difficult to see the world ruled by humans as what it truly was. However, in modern times where everyone was connected with each other, there was no shortage of the grime and filth that was publicized and broadcasted. Some of it was even heralded as an example of good. And now, when we are zooming through reality on a time warping track to the future, it is undeniable. I am flawed. We are flawed. We are imperfect. We are guilty. We have done wrong. But we have also done right. Pure evil does not exist within me as a person. Only the extremes of emotion and the misguided beliefs that accompany ignorance. Yes, there are those among me that have tried to act for the greater good. There are many who have feel into valleys and climbed out of the abyss and leapt up to the peaks of mountains. There were those who fell from grace. Good and evil is not as simple as it seems. The world and the actions of those who lived within it were not entirely black and white. We are all shades of gray, each and every one of us. The crimes committed in desperation, the deeds accomplished out of a wish to repent and escape from remorse, the progress that was gained by using the greed and worst qualities of people to motivate them. Do the ends justify the means? What is good and what is bad? Is there even such a thing? There were those who acted in good faith only to commit the most heartless atrocities. There were those who wanted the best for their countries. They followed their orders and by doing so, kicked in the wrong doors, bombed the wrong people, while saluting those who gave them their orders. It was all for a *good* cause. Without a doubt, we can feed the hungry, persuade the wicked, stop the wars, end the corruption, free the slaves, but there is more where that came from. As much good as there may be, there is also endless violence and much in between. What point is there in apologizing for something human civilization has experienced from the moment it was invented?

"But we must strive to be better," said the activist. "To dismiss the wrongdoings of the past as immutable human behavior is to give up. It is to say that humans are incapable of change. Wouldn't that be too tragic?"

Indeed, and what responsibilities does the one who placed us in this situation hold? Does their power or their omniscience excuse them from their actions? The atrocities and infractions committed towards us cannot go unpunished. This grudge must not be extinguished. What morals does an almighty being have that would convince them that such reprehensible cruelty was justified? Only one who is depraved or one who operates on a set of ethics completely foreign from us would consider any of this situation to be righteous. Whomever it is, it must be someone whose concept of life and death, time and space, and joy and misery is either completely different, or perhaps even absent. What would someone who knows not of mortal needs consider to be problematic? What type of culture would they have? Or is it simply that morality does not exist and is simply a human invention? It is as though we are looking at the world of humans from the viewpoint of an insect. Our world was one of purpose, of making the most of a life, of fulfilling our desires. It was not one of ant hills, pheromones, and the simple world of that which is pleasant and that which is not. But perhaps we give ourselves too much credit. Ants can move, communicate with each other, and respond to their environment. From the perspective of whomever did this, are we similar? I am not so sure. Are we the insects in this scenario, or are we the plants? Each and every one of us is confined to a certain duration of time. We could act upon anything before our birth, and we are unable to act upon anything after our demise. We are prisoners of the third dimension, unaware of what lies beyond. If an animal could move and a plant could not, are we the plants? Are we crops ready to be cut down once it is time to harvest? What about one level deeper? Are we animate or inanimate? Are we closer to the unmoving stones being worn down by the forces of time than we are to whomever did this to us? The answers to these questions are beyond us. Just as we do not know or care for the thoughts and dreams of rocks and boulders, so too could we be nothing more than a pebble in the river of higher dimensions. I want to tell those out there beyond the reaches of our perception that we have feelings, emotions, and hopes just as they do. Unfortunately, I do not know if they do have hopes and dreams. As much as we would like to think we matter, there is no evidence to support that. The idea that life is sacred, that death is divine, and that the human brain is the most complex thing in the universe is mere hubris. We have built our self-worth on hubris, and now it is falling apart like a stack of cards.

Who was it that told us that we were made in the image of God? Whichever god it was that we were made in the image of must truly be just as irresponsible and fickle as we are to leave us in this state. It is the work of a sadist to unilaterally create a mutation like this which strips us our autonomy. Judge, jury, and executioner, but no trial. Tell us our charges. Read us our Miranda rights. Give us due process. Assign us an attorney. How can a god be just if I am to suffer like this without knowing why? You can give us ten commandments, an eightfold path, five pillars, and other lists, but no amount of mixed signals will clear it up. I prayed for each and every one of you. I am owed at least that much. What have I been praying for if all of it only ended as this? It's a true shame.

All that time was wasted. It was all for nothing. If instead of worshiping such a disappointing entity that believed it could test us at any moment or time as a way for us to prove our worthiness, I wish that we could have spent all that time more productively. Imagine all of those stonings we could have avoided. All those beheadings that never needed to happen. No wars needed to be fought. No one needed to be burned at the stake. No ritual killings, fewer idols, less suffering, more truth. No angry mobs and riots. All the terrible deeds I did in the name of God may have never been needed in the first place. What a waste of time. What a waste of thought. What a waste of energy. Is this blasphemy? What does it matter if we have been forsaken? If there is an afterlife, would I change anything? Would I still think these thoughts? It depends on whether we desire an afterlife. After living in this purgatory of eternal gloom, spending another eternity anywhere else just seems like another unreasonable punishment. Whether it be heaven or hell, I am tired, very tired. I simply do not have it in me to do this again. If there was a heaven full of endless joy, that too will easily become boring. If an afterlife is a life of no change, then what difference does it have from this? Indeed, unlike a heaven or a hell that is artificial and designed to be one way or another, this may be better. This is arguably at least real. I may not ever be freed from this existence, but if I am and I was forced into an afterlife, what that would entail is that I would be limited to an existence where we have already lived our lives. Our ability to affect the mortal world has been taken away from us, and all we become are merely sheep grazing out at pasture. We trade our freedom and autonomy for either a fate of eternal pain and torture, or a fate where we live without freedom under the supervision of rulers we did not elect. It is a fate where we are cursed to watch over our successors make the same mistakes we did, have the same struggles. It is a fate where we realize that our role in the land of the living is one of the past and that anything of meaning or significance has been set in the past. It is a fate where we are confined to the retirement home of the formerly living, convincing ourselves that we are happy while having very little reason to believe so. If there are deities and realms of the dead, be they pleasant or detestable, perhaps we were the lucky ones to have escaped such a hopeless destiny.

We can very easily be thankful. However, I feel that to be grateful to be what I am feels as though I am surrendering. It feels as though I am giving up on ever escaping this existence. It feels as though whatever made us this way has won. And I don't want that. Whatever this ends in, I want it to end in either triumph or a burst of glory. Despite how bleak everything is, I can't simply give up. That would be admitting defeat. If all I needed to dig ourselves out of this hole was one more push, one more step, and I raised a white flag before taking it, choosing instead to spend the rest of time wallowing in self-pity, then that would make the trillions and quadrillions of years all the more tragic.

The story of Humanity should not be one of grief. It should be one of transcendence and endless drive for more. That is what Humanity should be remembered as.

CHAPTER 12: THE COLLAPSE

The advance of intelligent species throughout the universe, which was arguably an inevitability, was one thing that I was skeptical I would ever witness. However, the current state of my existence permitted me to see what would become of our galaxy whenever I was not lost in my own thoughts. This opportunity was an interesting practice in formulating hypotheses based on what I observed with the naked eye and then refining my perspective as new information was collected over the trillions of years. Although the odds were against each and every group that became capable of reaching space, we managed to bear witness to the blooming of a vibrant web of growth across the cosmos that was inspiring, perplexing, and the source of much envy.

Our first experience with the presence of aliens was in the form of probes that visited us periodically over the first tens of millions of years. It wasn't until billions of years had passed that we started seeing macro level changes at a higher frequency. Initially, it was simply a matter of seeing planets that had a certain luminescence that seemed unnatural and out of the norm. While many of these could have been the cause of complex chemical reactions, I believe that many of the rocky planets that I have seen were in fact inhabited by creatures that sensed visible light. Similar to how the earth once shined brightly in the darkness due to the presence of electric light illuminating our world, these other planets seemed to have similar properties like a candle in the dark night. Of course, when considering the pale blue dot, how easily can one make out artificial light within the great distances we traversed? Our notions of intelligent life in these early stages may have been misconceptions based on wishful thinking. However, what we would find later would turn our preconceptions on their head and provide a helping of credence to our imaginative daydreams.

The more advanced species built megastructures that were visible from space and some of these structures were even larger than planets. At some point, I imagine chemical rockets were too rudimentary, and they required larger structures that could help them reach orbit and siphon energy and resources from other parts of their solar systems. This must have been especially true for those worlds with higher gravity. In my travels, there was one planet I saw that was in the beginning stages of colonizing their system and going interstellar. It had an orbital ring around it that circled the equator. Meanwhile, at the Lagrangian point, where the gravitational pull between the planet and their sun was effectively the same, was a large grid that would fire out high powered lasers periodically. These lasers seemed to be directed at spaceships and propelled them using light to reach the outer portions of the system. Of course, to slow down, they needed to use some form of propulsion. It seems that the aliens realized this and had a solution in mind. When I exited this system, I saw a giant structure on the outer reaches of the system that was hundreds, maybe thousands of times larger than the laser grid near the sun. We think that where the laser grid near the sun was powered by solar and perhaps nuclear fusion, the grid at the outer reaches of this solar system was likely powered by a non-solar source. We believe that it was using cosmic background radiation instead, and somehow collecting all this energy using an incredibly large array. Although I am not sure why, I think they wanted a renewable energy source similar to the sun that did not require the maintenance of some form of fuel source. Surprisingly, even fusion or antimatter was not adequate. This was a civilization that was thinking in the long term. Their ambitions seemed to extend over millennia, to the outer reaches of their galaxy, and towards the end of the universe's lifespan.

Ambition, however, is not a rarity among the spacefaring generations of the various races that dot the cosmos, but culture and approach is. We were witness to another system that had similar megastructures and incredible engineering, but it was distinctive in that those aforementioned structures appeared to have been present for an extremely long period of time. Most structures like space elevators and space bridges, which were once thought impossible to construct in our time, have been bleached by solar radiation and broken into fragments due to impacts from space junk. Somehow the planets had their orbits altered to the point where their orbits were in perfect alignment, allowing for bridges to be made to connect the planets together. I do not understand how such alignments could be maintained in the long term when considering that the impact of the gravitational pull of moons and collisions from non-planetary bodies could easily misalign the configuration. Our conjecture is that whoever created these space bridges destroyed the moons and any asteroids or comets which could interfere with the space bridges while using the raw materials to construct these bridges. This allowed for what I saw to exist and to last. We do not know for sure, since we were too far to see clearly whether this was the case, and there were not enough clues to confirm the negation or affirmation of this theory. I do not know what it took to do this, or how long, but what is clear is that it must have taken a great deal of creativity to resolve to construct such an unconventional thing. I imagine with each revolution, the planets traveled across the system like the hand of a clock, ticking away along a two dimensional plane even after their creators were long gone. I wondered what could have happened for a civilization to go dark as this one has. Was it system level apocalypse, or were they spirited away? As I darted away from this system, I saw, out in the cold reaches of space far from any star, a large solar system sized object that did not match anything I have seen previously. It was a large metallic object with corridors and grooves that zigzagged along its length, forming labyrinths of metal. Is this where everyone went? Are they still there? I wished I could get closer, but I was going in the opposite direction. It was clear that it was artificially made. There was no way that it could have been the product of one or two solar system's worth of raw material. No. This appeared too dense to be created from a single system. Whatever created this must have been capable of interstellar travel at the very least. What is it for? I could only guess. In the end, I never figured out its purpose, or anything about it. The only thing I was sure of was that it was very old. As for how old, I cannot be sure, but it is possible that it is older than the human race. I could not tell what was happening within this object, but I did not see any activity from the distance I was viewing it at. We believe it was nothing more than ruins— the remains of a glorious empire. What happened here to lead to a civilization of such a level of advancement to disappear? Did they destroy themselves in some event? Famine is unlikely given their advanced nature. Did what happened to us happen to them? War is possible. However, if there was a war, I do not know what that would look like, or what clues and remnants that would leave. What does an interstellar war look like exactly? Is it loud and bombastic, or quiet and precise? How is it fought? Although I never found out the identity of this giant hunk of metal, I would learn well how interstellar wars are fought in the billions and trillions of years to come.

By this point, it became apparent that not only was there life throughout the universe, but there were also many intelligent species, some of which managed to become space faring. The spacefaring civilizations, while they may have been few when we landed on the moon and walked on Mars, became more widespread in the eras and epochs afterwards, growing in number and diversity. Not only were we living in a galaxy teeming with life, but we were living in a galaxy that acted as the playground of many intelligent species. Each of these held their own culture, their own views on life, and approached their growth and spread in different ways. For those that could communicate with each other upon contact, I imagine they would open lines of trade and collaborate on large projects. There is no way to know for sure, but the patterns of movement, and interactions between spaceships that appeared to have designs originating from differing schools of thought indicated a level of interplay between multiple species on an interstellar level. Of course, this is merely speculation. When all one can do is peer through a hole in a wall, it is the only option left. Granted, it is always possible that multiple intelligent species grew together and originated on the same planet, and thus were able to coexist from the beginning. However, I have no way of determining the accuracy or probability of such a supposition. We could only extrapolate from the observations that we made based on past experience, and in an existence where all I could do was observe and theorize without consequence, my imagination led me down multiple interesting realms of possibilities.

Sooner or later, I found myself questioning, given the nature of the large spans of distance between stars and systems and the way in which different systems travel throughout the galaxy, how can communication be handled effectively if it is limited to the speed of light? I am willing to bet that these civilizations have mastered the quantum realm and may be capable of using small artificially created wormholes to send messages. This would enable the flow of information to be instantaneous regardless of the distance and limitations imposed upon us by relativity. This means that communication between civilizations may actually be like our interactions over the internet: seemingly instant, overflowing with information, and effectively connecting multiple physical places in digital form. When the internet was made available to the average person, it allowed for a homogenizing of culture across the world where people could interact with each other regardless of the country that they were from. The main dividers seemed to be that of language and hardware. However, if a civilization has reached a sufficiently high level of advancement, then would it not be true that language would not be a barrier? Similarly, differences in hardware or technology can easily be remedied by providing the appropriate information regarding how to manufacture and improve hardware to allow for new functionality. The phenomenon of homogenization may not be limited to the tools of communication, but also perhaps physical bodies. If one can upload their minds, then it could easily be the case that two different species may eventually develop to have the same bodies through biological engineering or cybernetic augmentation. After all, if you do not need to be burdened with the tools provided to you through evolution, then would it not be the case that the most optimal physical form would be chosen? That would lead to the question of what is the most optimal form for a sentient being. As we've seen on Earth, there are certain forms that are better suited to some tasks than others. Therefore, it is unlikely that there is a physical form that would be the best at all tasks. What this means is, if a group has advanced far enough technologically, they may choose to have multiple bodies instead of one. It may be entirely possible for a single consciousness to control multiple bodies, or switch bodies in the way us humans may have changed clothes based on the occasion. Could an entire civilization consist of one consciousness? The idea seems a bit too centralized to be manageable. Naturally, the changing of bodies may be a more intimate and personal action than changing clothes are, since the body can influence how the mind behaves and reacts to the outside world. Although the brain controls the actions of the body, it is also true that in many multicellular organisms with a neurological system, the chemical processes of the body can determine and influence the development and behavior of the brain. Therefore, I believe it is not out of the question for a choice of body to also be a statement on the choice of mindsets and behaviors one wishes to exhibit. It could very easily be what the fashion of intelligent species evolves into after they reach a spacefaring status.

As might be expected, these speculations of homogeneity across civilizations and species are dependent upon finding common ground. I envisioned a galaxy of species trading with one another, forming unions, and organizations. Like the United Nations, the European Union, NATO, and other large blocs, I fantasized of creatures from many planets organizing into councils, laying down infrastructure for interplanetary travel and allowing tourists from other civilizations onto their planets to leverage their interstellar reach. Outsiders would be won over by their soft power and technological prowess and, in the process, their influence and reach would grow even further. Political structures that might have existed on Earth may exist here in space on a larger scale with more complexity and nuance. There may be factions and divisions where certain species align themselves militarily with others. If there can be factions, perhaps there can be empires as well. What would governments of the future look like? Generally speaking, in the earth's past, the larger a country was, the more difficult it was to govern. This was not only because of the physically larger land mass, but also because of the higher populations which typically contained more ethnicities and cultures. What about galactic empires and federations? If humanity's history is anything to go by, it seems almost impossible to govern a significant portion of the galaxy when people are involved. Not only is it necessary to police crime on planets, but also it is necessary to prevent it in space. Space, as we all know is massive, and it is impossible to be everywhere at once. If someone wants to commit a crime, smuggle goods, or start a rebellion, it may be very difficult to stop it. The only way governance on an interstellar level may be possible is through the use of technology and decentralized rule. Even with the presence of wormhole based communication, it will take at least light years to send forces to suppress rebellions if those wormholes are microscopic and cannot be used to transmit large amounts of physical matter. Similarly, if there are any disasters or urgent events, the ability of a centralized government to respond is highly limited by its physical distance from the event that is occurring. This is assuming that these civilizations cannot break past the wall of relativity. I have not witnessed such a thing, and I have not seen any ships flying into wormholes or even seen a wormhole which can enable shortcuts through space. Based on what I have observed so far during my travels, there is infrastructure that allows for near light speed travel in the form of laser grids being placed in most systems that have been colonized. These seem to function as a sort of interstellar super highway that uses either light or gravity to propel and direct spaceships in the general direction of their destination. If faster than light travel was a possibility, then it is plausible that it was not something I would have been able to witness with my eyes even if it did exist.

Will there eventually be a solution to such a problem? Perhaps, but what is quite clear to me is that any large factions that emerge within the galaxy will not take a form that is similar to any empires that we have seen in the past. If they do, it is obvious that such empires will not last long. While I can see the possibility of civilizations and races tearing across systems, pillaging and scorching planets as they travel through the cosmos, actual governance and long term settlements that can last millions of years without conflict will require a level of ingenuity and maturity from all life that are its citizens. If the history of the human race is anything to go by, all empires eventually fall, and it is solely the competence of the leaders and the sentiment of the citizens which seems to determine whether the fall is graceful or bloody and violent.

While I have not seen the expanse and reach of an interstellar civilization, what I have been able to bear witness to was the way in which more advanced civilizations would prey on others. It is said that there is always a bigger fish, but in space, size alone is not enough. Strategic savvy and technological superiority seems to be the deciding factor when it comes to battles in space. I have seen many ships become disabled from afar as their lights went out, and their propulsion zeroed out, leaving these large transport vessels floating in space on an uncontrolled trajectory. It seems that in space, destroying your enemies or your mark is taboo, or rather counterproductive.

What seems to hold value are intact goods, prisoners, and ships. As a result, it seems that the preferred method of capturing prey is one that leaves them in one piece. The predation of less advanced civilizations is likely not only limited to space, but also extends into the realm of planetary invasions. Much like the conquistadors, I can fathom the concept of travelers from spacefaring groups finding uncolonized planets and claiming these planets for themselves to use as they please. I estimate that when mankind was just beginning to escape Earth's gravity, such civilizations were few, making the first groups capable of interstellar travel the ones which carried out such invasions. This must have left civilizations that had yet to make first contact with the decision of whether to advertise their position to potential life in the universe, or to go radio silent. Indeed, there must have been some planets that managed to hold their own against the invaders for some time, but there also must have been others that have predicted the dangers of communicating on full blast. Later on, as more planets became colonized, we likely begin to see this reach a ceiling as races and civilizations arrived upon the cosmic borders they formalized for their interstellar territories.

If this was the case, then the increasingly ambitious nature of many of the inventions I saw acted as plausible evidence. Things I would have originally thought impossible or beyond the realm of intelligent life began to fill the skies. From bright systems powered by Dyson spheres and artificial moons to colonies and settlements on the edge of black holes, the ingenuity of intelligent life allowed for those who lived to use the power of stars and black holes to transcend space and time and manipulate the universe to their will. At the same time, in the later stages of the universe before the stars went dark, I saw the aftermath of space based life. These organisms fed off of the space dust and whatever was available in space to reproduce and fill the empty space with biological matter. Like the plants that filled the empty ocean floors and colored the earth green, these extremophiles (or perhaps astrophiles) were capable of surviving in a vacuum in a range of temperatures. If it were not for the expansion of the universe, I believe these creatures would have spread through the cosmos like a virus and supplanted the status quo. Fortunately, they did not, and I could enjoy the fruits of advanced civilizations without limit till the end.

The end, if it could be called that, was gradual. It was a slow process that took place over trillions of years and was a long period of turbulence, uncertainty, and a slow dying. It was like watching a sick, old man with labored breathing fight to live when a quick, merciful end might have been for the best. As time passed, the civilizations that kept pace on my journey began to drop away. Some of them were wiped out in wars where they fought over the empty region of space that I occupied. These wars were not dissimilar to watching ants and insects fight. It was, from a distance, like watching large armies in intricate geometrical shapes change configuration over and over until one side was no longer left. If I had to liken it to something, it was like watching a game of Go. However, where Go might be played by two players on a flat board with a grid, this was a game with far more complexity. It was a game with trillions or even quadrillions of players, an endless, continuous grid, and it took place in at least three dimensions. The strategic foresight on each and every spaceship, on each army, was something that would make the most intelligent human seem as smart as a rock and I imagine the toll was something that would make the worst of humanity's past atrocities against their fellow man seem peaceful or merciful in comparison.

Then there were the eccentric. Some of those who were not wiped out in war wasted their resources building strange, functionless structures wherever I went as though they were planting flags. These were beautiful and intricate pieces that seemed to have artistic value, but art is a very subjective thing. It had the sophistication of Roman architecture while at the same time an organic and spontaneous feeling like a Jackson Pollock painting. Stylistically, it seemed to transcend themes and messages that we were familiar with. Whether something was lost in translation, or it was simply the difference between an ant and a God, I understood nothing other than that I should be in awe. Whenever light shown upon these designs, I could remember that I was not alone, and have a sense of calm that I had not felt since the time I was born. It was a feeling of congeniality, of adoration, of love. I did not comprehend what compelled these beings to chase after me, but I was thankful. I was thankful that they did and that they stayed with me for all these years, sacrificing their livelihoods. This too, like all good things, had to end. The last that were with me lost pace, slowing down and taking distance with every century and millennia. They were losing ground against the current of time. Eventually, they were so far away I could not see them. I recall being in the dark and hoping that they were still there, just past my range of vision. However, I knew at some point that they would run out of energy and disappear into the darkness never to be seen again. The worship of the greatness of existence acts as a reminder of its eventual close.

As the stars died, and the universe returned to blackness, I understood then that the luxuries I enjoyed up to that point would never return. My universe was dead, and what was left of it was a corpse that would rot away until nothing was left.

CHAPTER 13: STRANDED

In a sense, we are all born alone, live alone, and die alone. This is the predicament of all life. The presence of others is merely a distraction from this fact. There is nothing here but me. The thoughts I think are mine. You standing there before me is only of significance if I notice you and acknowledge your presence. Otherwise, your existence is diminished. If you were out of my sight, and I did not hear you or notice your influence on my world, you would effectively not exist to me for that moment. We are all isolated from one another. This is a double edged sword. On one hand, you have a sense of privacy, and by keeping yourself separated from others, you can generate a unique identity. This identity is one that can only be created by oneself, but can be influenced by others. The higher the influence of others, the less of a unique identity you will have. This is the price that needs to be paid to recognize oneself as an individual with their own set of distinguishing qualities.

This was true in the days we were mortals. It is only more poignant now, just in a somewhat twisted form. Other planets have had civilizations that rose and fell, but were never cursed or never observed to be cursed. These civilizations never understood me. I only understood them at a surface level. We were as separate and distant as strangers passing by in a crowded street. Although we never truly knew one another, I was sorry to see them go. It was like those moments where the bar or café that I frequented eventually became another home. I was a regular and at some point, when I was not lost in my drink, I noticed the other regulars. Despite not speaking or knowing anything about them, the days that they were not there were the days that felt off. I would overhear their conversations, and they would overhear mine. I would gradually understand their usual schedules and could predict when they would enter through the front door. I would go in, and see the same bartender or barista, and at some point, they would remember my name and my usual orders. Then, one day, I would come in like I usually did, and they were simply gone, and it was not for a single day. Sometimes it would be death, other times, life takes them to other places. I could call out "Come back," but they were already gone. Though my memories of them will remain, if we were to meet again, it would not be through the usual means.

Their ends are likely different from my end. They met their deaths in ways that seemed to be either under their control or the consequences of their actions. Whether they died with a bullet to the head, cancer, or simply shot themselves in the foot and bled out, all can be traced back to their actions in some way. In the midst of the growing scarcity within the universe, those who met their ends found troubling ways to go about it. There were those that seemed to choose to destroy themselves in a form of self-imposed genocide. I witnessed one planet do it, and later saw the aftermath on the far reaches of the domain of their sovereign rule. Rather than a single leader deciding and wiping out all life, each planet belonging to this civilization destroyed itself with weapons of mass destruction. They could clearly go on for millennia afterwards, but they felt compelled to end it then and there, leaving working machinery that did not rot and never became idle to toil for the rest of eternity while their corpses decomposed. It could have been the case that they realized that their end could have been one of the most noble of missions. It could have been one of the greatest sacrifices. Alternatively, it could have merely been the only escape. It could have been a mercy for those who survived: feed off my dead husk so that at least you may have a chance to live and tell the tales of our glory.

The others who fought and fought to the dying end seemed to be the ones to either achieve immortality and escape, or the first to die. As though realizing that there was a choice between endless struggle and finding a solution at the risk of ending an empire, they chose the route that ventured to thrash against the forces of nature before they too would join the darkness. In doing so, they expended resources, lives, and quenched their suns, squeezing out every drop of energy they could in the hopes that they could reach the finish line of Samsara and become reborn in another time or another reality where they would no longer need to suffer. It was not to be, and they too would vanish. First it would be one planet, then the system, each bastion of life going dark. One at a time, like flames being quietly extinguished. Each planet died alone. Each individual in that empire died in their own unique way, but they died nonetheless. Was it worth it? To die in that way? Is it worth it to continue to live in misery and pass long after nothing is left? Only the dead can tell, and they're long gone. The ones who are left will either leave this universe for greener pastures or will meet similar ends. All that is left here are ashes, voids, and nothing on the horizon. You can choose your destination, but you can't see it. Discovery, exploration, conquest: pointless when all the fields you find are barren.

Just as my life is my own, so too is my experience. We are alone in our suffering. There are no others. I am the only one doomed to wander the universe for all eternity. This is what I believe. If there were others, I have not seen them. If there were others, even if I spend the remainder of the universe watching for them, it is doubtful that I would ever find them. In the darkness, they may effectively have never existed. What if there was no darkness? What if I could see everything without needing to strain myself? Even then, it is unlikely that I would ever find them. Each galaxy is vast. The observable universe is even more vast. This observable universe which consists of clusters, superclusters, and more has a scale that is beyond human understanding. You could see a number describing its size and not fully understand it due to lacking the context. It is massive. However, this is a meager speck within the unobservable universe that lay beyond all light that had a chance to travel before me. This unobservable universe and everything inside of it is expanding. It is expanding so rapidly that the remnants of massive superclusters become measly islands within the spaces between, oases within a hostile reality. You may venture out into the unknown at your own discretion, but unless you can effortlessly traverse distances on a scale that dwarfs galaxies, clusters, and the former observable universe, then you will simply be setting out to die a meaningless demise with little hope of rescue. Indeed, if there were others just like me, they would be trapped within their predetermined paths, blindly stumbling through an empty reality. A meeting is never meant to be.

This leaves the poor souls I took with me. Like all things, I had taken them for granted until the day they were gone despite understanding their eventual fate. However, unlike the life that proliferated throughout the cosmos, these were special. They were mine. They were there for me. If it was not for me, they could have spent their finite time in a more meaningful way. For that, I feel deeply remorseful. I had nothing to offer them, and yet they stayed by my side. What were they thinking? Why follow me? I asked and asked, but my voice never reached them. When I first made their acquaintance, I noticed that they had receiver-shaped structures like antennae directed towards me. I asked myself whether they were listening. Maybe they were trying to hear me, but I was simply not loud enough. It could have been that they did hear me, but they simply did not understand. If they did, why did they not send something back? Why did we not communicate? Or was it simply that while they could communicate, I was not able to hear them? The endless spiral of blame that I fall within never seems to stop dragging me deeper into the abyss of incomprehension. I did not understand them, their purpose, or who they were. They did not understand me, otherwise we should have been able to communicate. It was a lost opportunity. I felt for them. They remember a time when the universe was more abundant. I made them waste their moments of youth and follow me into these times of desolation, and all I could do was watch. It was like watching a sick patient, like someone you love passing away, wasting slowly. You would want to do everything, but you don't know what you should do, or even what you can do. Their fate is out of your hands.

Is this what it truly means to be alone? To have nothing but your own thoughts to hold you close? At times it does not sound too bad. As humans, we did not always need others to live. Although our identities as social creatures have been coded into our genes, there has been value in each and every one of us being able to function as individuals who are capable of being self-reliant when the time calls for it. I can scarcely recall the feel of another person, but I yearn for it. I just wish to be held in another's arms, to be separate from others with my own thoughts but still together in spirit. The tactile sensation of another person's skin, the emanation of warmth radiating through human contact. The understanding that we are separate individuals brought together is one that I cannot stop longing for. You do not need others to live, and yet it hurts to be without them, like holding your heart over a vat of liquid nitrogen and feeling it gradually freeze into a hard mass of flesh that can easily shatter when dropped. Simultaneously, the presence of others can be like holding your heart over an open flame and feeling it slowly turn to cinders like your personality is being eroded away bit by bit.

Others can be hurtful and unforgiving. They can insult you, reject you, and deny you of any dignity at a moment's notice. To be able to trust, we must have relationships that are built on a foundation of trust. However, trust is difficult to build and easy to destroy. Often, backstabbing and treachery have even been rewarded and have been a strategic and pragmatic choice. One moment you are a friend, and the next, you are a stepping stone. The whims of humans are fickle, and betrayal and shame can be directed towards you without warning. This is the nature of human relationships. There is the experience of being cheated and the experience of cheating. Selfishness and ego dominate our actions. We have lived lives of much pride, but also much shame, and that made us flawed creatures. The identities we built for ourselves were unfortunately dependent upon the opinions of others. By doing so, our identities become an extension of society and those around us rather than an extension of ourselves. This leaves those who are unable to fit in a dire predicament. The pain of not fitting in is one that imprints itself as trauma and can last a lifetime. It can build and build to destructive effect. Then there are those of us who fit in, but understand that they have nothing in common with their fellow man. They are there, mixed within the crowds, but they are not the same as everyone else. They are an outsider wearing one face in public and wearing another in private. They do this not to deceive, but to survive. Yes, if you are different, you become the nail that sticks out only to be hammered down. It is easier to live a safe life than a daring one. It is better to exhibit the qualities that society values rather than qualities that may result in an objectively more fulfilling livelihood. We have no choice but to do this. If not, we are recognized as worthless, as the scum of society. They become the abandoned goods lining the streets who need to be thrown away. If you cannot exhibit your value, you only exhibit the reasoning for your disposal. As a result, we all live lives we do not wish to. We turn our backs on who we are and who we think we are meant to be and give up on our dreams. Our ancestors learned the sciences and the maths so that we could supposedly learn the arts. Their ancestors fought wars so that their descendants could learn the sciences. This was how it was meant to be. Each generation was to leave a better life for their descendants. However, the wars never stopped. The ties between generations degraded. Society never advanced, and people never grew beyond the practice of exhibiting their value as individuals. The great things we were meant to do were never in the plans. No, we were only cattle to be slaughtered, walking the paths we were told to walk. Indeed, if it were not for others, we may have lived the lives we wanted. In the past, this may not have been the disadvantage we thought it was, because our actions were contributing to our survival. However, in a time of plenty, in a time when scarcity was no more, we continued regardless of how unreasonable. Yes, whenever we fixed a problem, we would introduce another in its place. It was all systems of control that continued endlessly, depriving us of ourselves, and turning relationships into feeding frenzies where everyone became emotional vultures preying on one another when they were at their most vulnerable.

We were never meant to build utopias where people can coexist peacefully. We were not designed for that. We were meant to survive the forces of nature. Anything beyond that is simply extraneous. All we were meant to do was to handle any obstacle that came our way, get a leg up on any and all competition, and leave behind offspring that would be doomed to do the same thing. Even if we built utopias, how long can such a thing stay intact? All civilizations rise and fall. People grow greedy, and the cycle of misery continues. The utopias that celebrate our individuality rather than use our individual nature as a way to force responsibilities that were no longer needed would never last. We can say that one day we could have lived in a time when others would not have stomped on our creativity and imposed their views on our identities, race, sexualities and backgrounds. We could say that we could have grown into agreeable individuals even with the presence of others. However, one does not discover the evils of the world by living in isolation.

Love could be a silver lining. Love, especially that which is unconditional, can be a support in the hardest of times. But whether there truly is such a thing as unconditional love is questionable. Conversely, it could also be considered to be foolishness - as trust is self-imposed weakness and vulnerability. You can love yourself, but that has a distinctive difference from the love of others. The feeling of appreciation from others, the need to depend on one another can provide a purpose where there was none. But what if that was only a smokescreen? What if that was only meant to be a distraction for simple-minded people like us so that we do not realize that we are more alone than we realize? It is a disheartening thought that forms in the absence of absolute confidence. It is also a thought that has a stronger empirical basis than a naive notion that love can conquer all. There is much of me that wishes not to think of it, and oftentimes, I do not.

It is also a topic that is very rarely broached in conversation. Ah! There is another silver lining: conversation and interplay. The marriage of minds in the exploration of ideas: collaboration, cooperation, confluence, and maybe even a shared mission. The ability to share your thoughts and incorporate ideas completely alien from anything you may consider yourself. It could be argued that ideas are living organisms themselves. Like us, they too grow and adapt to their environments. They change based on advancements in topics or can wither and die as a topic is changed or another idea gains a greater hold on the attention of individuals. These thoughts and figments of our imagination are also, like other humans, our offspring.

If thoughts were individuals, then they obey laws of natural selection as well. They can reproduce through the collaboration of two human minds, or can be brainstormed by a single person: sexual and asexual reproduction. However, without us, they would simply wither away. I wonder, how many ideas are out there lost to the march of time? How many ideas are out there that we have yet to think of? Surely it must be infinite. Sometimes thoughts repeat themselves, but occasionally a unique idea can form under unique conditions. I wonder, do you need to be intelligent or even sentient to form a thought? Is it possible for an inanimate stone or even the universe to have thoughts of the future, to form ideas? Perhaps their manifestation of a thought is in the physical form. The decision to form planets, the decision to expand. These all follow laws, but there is a certain level of randomness, of stochasticity, mixed into the process. What happens is predictable to some extent, but not necessarily predetermined. There is still the opportunity for interplay. Perhaps, we too are thoughts and ideas dreamt up by the universe—memes born out of a being that operates on a far greater timescale. Maybe we were simply those in a long line of thoughts and ideas that were manifested by this creature. It could have been that in the moments after the big bang, there was life completely alien to us, based on sub-atomic particles and energy instead of molecules, which lived and died on the matter of nanoseconds that may have had simple thoughts. I wonder, if those creatures lived in our time, would they have found it to be an unbearable slog as we find this time to be to us? To find out, could we ask the universe? Maybe, but would the universe know the answer or be aware of it? Like we are unaware of the activities and actions of our cells, we could simply be too insignificant to even be considered a thought. We might just be like a neural activation, the beginnings of a thought, but not quite the end product. We may just be a process in a long line of processes.

At the beginning, the thoughts of the universe may have been simple: grow, expand, consume, explore. As it grew more mature, its thoughts grew in complexity and became more abstract: form, gather, think. Now, what is it thinking? Are its thoughts more like that of an Alzheimer's patient with vast distances and vague memories of what it once was, or is there more to come? Is there a complexity within this emptiness that is beyond human understanding? Is there something wonderful hidden within the quadrillions and quintillion years to come? Will there be conversations with other realities and universes to create new ones? Is there a way to find out? At this time, in this moment, the only one I can ask is the universe itself. If the universe could speak back, maybe I would not feel so alone. Maybe we can engage in conversation, create new ideas, and grow into something new and different. If the universe could speak back, maybe it would be my friend.

Maybe it already is, and I just have not realized.

CHAPTER 14: NO MORE CHANCES

It is like the last dance in a ballroom. You take your partner's hand and either lead them or are led in response to the music that echoes through the lavish hall. There is a rush of euphoria that gives you momentum with each step you take that matches the beat and changes in the song accordingly. It is not only a conversation between yourself and your partner, but also between yourselves and the musicians performing at the front of the hall. The more sophisticated and difficult the movements, the greater the sense of accomplishment. Before you know it, the song is already over. You ask for one more dance, but you find yourself reaching your hand out to someone who is no longer there. Old age has caught up. Your joints ache, and rheumatism prevents you from matching the rhythm. The music is gone. The lights are extinguished, and the light pouring in from the outside has been replaced by moonlight. The dance you just finished was the last one, and there will never be another one or another one like it. That was the last dance. Did we make the most of it?

The future is still to come. There is still the chance for possibilities and opportunities. But we know that those will vanish. Time ticks on. For us mortals bound by time, sense, and reflex, this experience that we are registering has already happened. By the time we recognize a moment to be the present, it no longer is. Enjoy the moment for it is already over. The more we understand this, the more it comes to light that the future is a past waiting for us to cognitively register it. In this sense, all that will happen already has, and we are passive observers trying to react despite operating on a time lag. The future is happening right now. The present has passed, and the past is all we know.

There are no more chances, no more redoes. The time for that has long passed. Did we do what we wanted prior to this? Did we leave our former lives behind satisfied? Of course not. There were still books we wanted to read and books we wanted to write. There were paths I wanted to walk and places that I wanted to see. There were chances that I did not take in the past that I hoped to take in the future. Of course those leaps of faith and chances will never come. It's too late. I can no longer face the fears I had and step bravely into the darkness to light the path ahead. All the people I wanted to meet and know better... Yes, everyone is here already. There is no one left out. But it is not the same. It is not the same where there is just me, and everyone else is merely a part of me like many thoughts in a single head fighting for supremacy over my mind. Each part of me tells me that he or she is more interesting, that they matter more and their ideas have more significance. It simply is not the same when you are in a crowded cell, suffocating and struggling for air.

Of course, there are things I still wished to do. There were cravings that lasted the eons that I want to put to rest. There are dreams I held that will need to go unfulfilled. But those dreams are not the ones I found to be the most tragic. No. It was the ones that were crushed under the weight of reality. It was the ones that had to be abandoned or suppressed so that I could live in an unforgiving world. It was the scenes where I discarded the person I thought I was meant to be and became another person instead. Looking back upon those moments is like watching us become strangers to ourselves. We no longer knew who we were, and gradually forgot the significance of our aspirations. We would keep telling ourselves, "If I save enough money, if I do this or that... then I can finally do the things I truly enjoy." It was the regrets I had while on Earth that strike back the hardest now that I am on the other end of the supercluster. Even when I was aware of the things I regretted, I was unable to do anything. Now, I do not even have the choice.

I imagined myself going back in time to fix the things I believed needed fixing. I would look back upon the lives that were squandered in the pursuit of meaningless tasks and try to find the moments that would have changed everything. There were the crucial turning points where a single decision here or there could forever change the trajectory of our lives. We would tell ourselves that if we had one more chance, then we could do things right. Even in a dog-eat-dog world, if I knew what fate I would receive if I did not make the right decision, I could have rebelled. I could have tried harder. I could have leapt further, ignored the risks, and followed my heart. I would have overcome my cowardice and latched onto the destiny I wanted with the tightest grip I could muster. The lives that ended in banality could be redeemed. I could have salvaged the broken lives and turned them into stars that lit up those around them like the kindling of society. I could have done all of that... if I had one more chance.

Life is fragile. Any day could have been our last. I should have taken more risks, acted with more urgency, and acted with more immediacy. I could have loved more. I could have been loved more. I could have had more friends and more meaningful interactions. I could have placed myself in the right places at the right times. I could have gotten that promotion or started that company. That would have made me happy. Or would it have? There was so much I lost in the drive to be more productive, and yet at the same time, there was so much I could have gained by increasing my productivity. The constant struggle between doing more and doing less is one of living to create a better future and enjoying a present while it is still there. Which is better? I do not know. All I want is to be happier, and yet, I do not know what that even means. Happiness never lasts. If it did, we would grow complacent. Despite that, what does happiness matter if it is fleeting? Does it matter at all, or is it purely a mirage in an emotional desert. We are simply vagabonds meandering through life, trying to chase the closest thing that can satisfy us. It does not matter if doing so takes us further away from a true escape or further away from fulfillment. We cannot see what is beyond the horizon. So, instead, we do what we think is best with limited information, trading the long term gratification for immediate satisfaction only to realize that doing so was making us stray further away from the lives we wanted to live.

It is as though there are three versions of us wandering a perilous maze. One rushes through without thinking of the dangers only to meet their end quickly. One avoids risks regardless of how small, and ultimately starves after being unable to take a single step forward. One observes the others, thinks, and then acts. The one who starves lives longer, but suffers till the end. The one who took on all risks suffered little, but did not live long. The one who was pragmatic lived long and suffered little as he understood that risk was relative when placed within a particular context. However, that version of us could only act on the information we had at the time. If we were to meet our end due to conditions which were out of our control, we too would perhaps regret our actions. In the end, we cannot be all versions of ourselves, and we will remain dissatisfied. As we watch our choices develop into outcomes, the lack of perfection rots us from the insides. The flaws stand out, and the victories are nothing more than expected. Those who survived till the end were the ones that wish their suffering ended longer or its nature was changed while those who did not last wish that they could have lived on despite whatever suffering and horror may be in store. In the end, we realize too late that our expedition to keep our heads above water and away from the abyss was meaningless.

The things we love will be perverted into something else. Everyone we know will die. Nothing is permanent, and even if we were given a second chance, that would not change. Even if we made the right decisions, nothing would change. We would still ask for a second chance. That is the curse of being an inhabitant of the future and a prisoner of the past: hindsight. Nothing is perfect, and it is impossible to be so. We can make the right decisions, act optimally, and follow our principles. However, in the end, we will lust after the path not traveled. The grass beyond the horizon is greener. The mirage in the distance is lush and inviting. In the hall of mirrors, the worlds behind each mirror are far more enticing than the world we are in. Whether we have no more chances, or an infinite number of chances, it's all the same. Time has passed and our mind has wandered around in mental circles. We had these very same thoughts before haven't we? You might be able to change your future actions to some degree, but unless you can turn back the clock, the past is set in stone.

PART 3

Throes of a Curse

CHAPTER 15: THE BLACK HOLE ERA

After the decay brought on by the Degenerate era, we now are witness to the Black Hole era. The era takes place in excess of a duodecillion years after the big bang. The sun has risen and now it has set. Twilight approaches. It is an era characterized by a cold and lonely universe that is not dissimilar from that of a rotting corpse. As the remnants of stars from white dwarfs to neutron stars to brown dwarfs decay, the light of the cosmos is snuffed out leaving only black holes to rule the universe. In this universe, subatomic particles are no longer able to coalesce to form matter, instead separating and falling apart due to proton decay. Matter itself has become an affront to the forces of physics and is exorcized from reality wherever such decay can no longer be kept at bay. The song heard passing throughout the universe is that of a requiem.

In this universe without stars and light, there is very little heat as well. The warm embrace of the bright bodies that birthed us is forever gone. We see now a period where everything is far enough away that new interactions between bodies of matter are limited to those that managed to keep within their gravitational wells and avoid being knocked away from their gravitational neighborhoods. That is, of course, assuming that such matter has yet to decay which is very unlikely. The new reality is now one of those wandering through the vastness unable to find friends, family, loved ones, or even strangers before decaying where they stand. There is almost nothing left except for black holes, and with the absence of light and heat, the presence of these can only be noticed upon approaching such bodies. For that which is still intact despite the forces of proton decay, once such gravitational forces are noticed, it is too late and any matter is swallowed up by the beasts which dominate the dying cosmos.

In time, even these beasts will die a hopeless death. They will leak Hawking radiation and eventually evaporate, leaving behind no traces in the spaces where they once tyrannically enjoyed their lives of extreme gluttony. However, that is a story for another era. In this time, we see life hang by a thread. New biological life may be feasible, however it is so unlikely that the chances of primordial life growing in the forms that we are most familiar with are effectively zero. No, the only life here is the life that was lucky enough to be born before everything started to deteriorate. This life never had the chance to escape the universe, and as a result, all they could do was struggle till the end. They clung onto whatever energy they could squeeze out of this reality through a mastery of particle physics. This meant that life took on a form that fed on the black holes that remained. They effectively walked a tightrope, using the gravitational forces and the radiation emitted by black holes to keep entropy at bay and sustain their lives. It was a balance between being close enough to the black hole to consume what they needed while also staying outside its grasp so as to not fall within. While the civilizations that managed to do this had this down to an exact science, the pure difficulty involved makes human accomplishments such as reaching orbit or landing on the moon seem absolutely mundane. Naturally, when life is at stake, life tries to find a way no matter the cost.

It is a strange situation to be in where the appropriate amount of risk must be taken, but what little one has is too valuable to give up. It was both an existence of pure daring, but also one of bondage. Among the millions of civilizations that remained to the end, the ones that managed to escape the universe and make their way out numbered less than ten. If the civilizations before were those who stayed within a burning building as a way to stay warm, the escapees were the ones who managed to rush out the front door or jump out of a window. Indeed, to find a way out in this situation required the stars to align. No, it required more than that as there are no stars left. Hel is cold. The moments before the end are colder. It already took great ingenuity to live next to a black hole. To go further, it takes incredible luck and greater ingenuity to use your only lifeline as a method to transcend your current reality. Those who managed to make their exit utilized their black holes as engines to travel across dimensions. To do so was an act that required a plunge, an act of great risk that not all civilizations were willing to take or were capable of even considering. Indeed, many of those who made their way out were at rock bottom with nowhere else to turn. With nothing to lose, they looked towards their master of life and death— the black hole— and decided to unlock the monster in the cage. The method by which each civilization did so was slightly different, but among the thousands who did so, the few that were able to tame the monster were able to conquer time and space and navigate a higher dimensional landscape as they pleased with some minor caveats.

These pioneers were the small minority that managed to make their legacy eternal. They were the ones who would live on to tell the story of their former home. However, the majority became a part of the graveyard that was the universe. In this graveyard, if anything is left, it is hard to find. All the bodies have either decayed, or have been swallowed into black holes. Simply put, there is no evidence anyone has ever lived in this universe. There are no dents left in the sky. There are no legacies left behind for others to find. The flood came, and there was no ark. The tombstones are missing, and the graves are gone. All that is left is a grave keeper with nothing to do. It blindly walks its rounds through the grounds day and night, while dreaming of times far gone in the past and of places that either no longer exist or never have. It makes its way from mausoleum to empty grave, trapped forever within the endless cemetery that is our infinity.

CHAPTER 16: THE VOICES IN OUR HEAD

Enough time has passed to the point that we are stunned that my mind has not already turned to mush like a form of synaptic retrogenesis. Humans have an intellect that barely allows them to process a century's worth of information, but this is far beyond that. Perhaps it had already become mush from the moment we became one being. The line between the sane and the insane is thin, indistinct, and vague. Maybe we were all certain levels of insane, and together we created this complete mess of a person. Regardless, I have managed to maintain some semblance of human thought that can be described with words. As to how long that will be the status quo is questionable, but I think that I am at my breaking point. The voices in my head don't stop, and I can no longer trace them back to the original personality that they belong to. They just echo back and forth, talking about everything from the mundane to the freakish. From one conversation between two disembodied voices discussing the weather and the rate of inflation to conversations about tumors and how to control groups of people within a cult, the topics are erratic and lack logical ties. It is as though I am being unwound into multiple people who are no longer who they used to be. Sometimes the voices are loud, sometimes they are soft, but they are very rarely silent. I can usually hear them, and whenever I think they are about to fade into the background, they come back. It is as though the source of the voices can read my mind. Of course they can. They are me.

"Is that an object approaching? What was that flash of light? I can't be the only one seeing that right?"

It is only through the well trained mental fortitude that I built through the eras and a certain level of desensitization that I can filter these voices out. However, the moment I relax, the noise begins to come back. True relief, it seems, is no longer a luxury that I can afford. When I direct my attention outwards, I find that there is little I can gather to anchor myself to reality. There is no light, no sound, and I have lost all sense of the speed that I am traveling at. When everything is pitch black, it is as though you have your eyes closed. However, when you have your eyes closed, you have the option of opening them. In our case, I am deprived of all sensory details, as though I was in a sensory deprivation tank for unimaginable periods of time until all my nerves have degenerated and everything has gone numb. This state of nothingness has gone on long enough that I can no longer tell if anything we experienced in the past has actually happened, or if I am simply remembering events, real and imagined, to cope with the current reality. If I take a method of deductive inference, then we could take the clues and signals that I can observe and use them to extrapolate to the past to learn how I arrived at where I am. However, there are no clues here. There are no signals, and no breadcrumbs. Only me.

The trail has gone cold eons ago. Now, all I am is a disembodied consciousness that effectively does not even exist and interact with an environment. I am like those artificial intelligences and simulations that existed within the world of circuits and transistors. I may as well be a brain in a vat of fluid. There is only some initial input in the form of memories. The rest is something we need to figure out on our own. It is interesting how in the past I remember, I felt so sure that I lived many lives as different people and that the universe we lived in was real. The limited senses I had acted as the foundations for us to build our sense of confidence. The times when I felt as though I was experiencing reality felt so short compared to the eternity of nothing that followed. That feeling, however warped it may be, has some basis in truth as the time of stars is over and will never return. Despite having an imperfect perception of the world, we placed so much importance on our senses, and now that they are gone, we have nothing to base our perception of reality upon. We can say that we think and therefore we are, but the very nature of our existence is a mystery. Do we take our memories at face value to represent what the past was, or do we scrutinize them to find holes in their construction? If we choose the latter, then how can we distinguish between memories that are inconsistent with reality, and memories that are flawed due to the passage of time which numbs the sharpest of pains and relegates each past event into a homogenous blur? The tools of reasoning we have at our disposal are deteriorating, and as time passes, our state of mind robs us of our ability to reason and cope with our reality. This was true when we supposedly walked the earth, but it is truer now.

"How bad could letting go be? If fighting against the current is so hard, then why not simply lose our grip on reality? Reality does not matter anymore. Why cling to it?"

The scientific method, of which we can use to derive answers about reality, has turned its back on us. We no longer live in a place where there are independent variables and dependent variables. Here, there are no variables except us. We are the one and only. We can change how we think, but outside of that, there is nothing left to act upon even if we could act upon it. Free will means nothing if there is nothing to act on. We are now living statues, petrified in place. Our eyes are covered in stone lids, and we cannot open them. The phantom limbs we so desperately worked to move and feel are now pointless. The time we wasted in search of that which was never there will never come back, and all the progress made is meaningless in the face of a universe we cannot influence.

The voices tell me it will be okay. Sometimes they urge me on, and other times, they stomp my aspirations into the ground in a bout of emotional whiplash. It does not matter whether things will be okay or whether everything is hopeless. We lose the moment we take the statements at face value. However, in this lonely place with no one else around, these voices are the only other thing out here that I can treat as someone else. They are the wall I can bounce my ideas off of. That is an opportunity that seems all too enticing at times. Perhaps there will come a day when I let go and begin to engage in conversation with these voices. However, that day is not today. I am still aware of who we are and who we are not and, the moment we take the plunge, that distinction ceases to be as apparent as it is now. In a world of nothing, the smallest crumb appears appetizing. Despite this, whether I like it or not, I have managed to create a foundation of self-control. Rather, it is a mindset of asceticism that comes not from limiting myself, but instead from being heavily deprived. When I know that nothing I do will fulfill my desires or needs, the very nature of taking actions and breaking discipline is an impossibility. I have nothing, and I will gain nothing. Whether this situation is good or bad is completely relative, and completely up to me. I learned this lesson well back when there was still light in this universe, and over time I retreated into the depths of my mind.

My sense of self is only vaguely human now. It has become more of an idea of a person rather than a person with identifiable features. I have become a shadow. The real me is somewhere else. Maybe the real me can be found, but with each second that passes, that person slips out of our grasp. What we are now is an amalgamation of qualities that transcend the physical. Whenever I picture myself, I do not see a humanoid bipedal body, but rather a pinkish silhouette that changes colors based on my mood. When I become angry, it becomes pointed and jagged with rough edges. When I become calm, it turns fluid and amorphous, like water accumulating into a human shaped puddle. It is as though I am an elemental force of nature. Sometimes, I am a discrete particle. Other times, I am a fluctuating wave. With such a mindset, the qualities of cultural exchange and social transactions mutate as well. Where one could base their identity off of a hometown or location on the earth which was complete with its own local cuisine, architecture, way of life, language, and practices, such identities no longer have any significance. I am no longer a child in the Chinese countryside, or a businessman in a bustling American city with skyscrapers running along the horizon. I am now whatever I choose to be. I have lived many lives, and took on the roles of many people. I have thoroughly traced the possible futures of each person, the interactions they might have had with other parts of me, and how they may have chosen to live. In the process, I have memories of lives I have only imagined outnumbering the lives that I have actually lived. This is trillions upon trillions of possibilities. Furthermore, these lives are not limited to those lived on Earth or even in this universe. Can a human mind handle all of that? I do not know. All I know is that I had enough time to become lost within the sea of information that I generated by myself.

Within these virtual worlds manufactured inside my head, the lives of humans gradually became boring. It was not as though I completely abandoned living such lives in my daydreams, but it was more that the humanity within these lives were gradually becoming unrelatable. The human part of me kept returning to these moments that never happened while the intellectual within me grew to take on its own personality that abstracted away from the things that made us human. I would rush to the climax, skip the buildup, and edit out the boring parts. My sense of humor had already been somewhat twisted and warped towards the avant-garde due to the vibrant meme culture of the internet era, but humor in this day and age has become something else. Vast expanses of empty space have become personified. They take on personalities and play a role in my jokes.

"Hello, I used to be a supercluster. After becoming an alcoholic, I became divorced from my universe and now pay alimony to a quasar. Look at how my standards have dropped."

"Here is a disembodied head whose body is gradually being formed out of stardust. Be careful. If you form a star, you'll stand out of the crowd."

"Woe is me. I don't even have two protons to rub together. My boss is rolling in antimatter, but for some reason, I don't get a raise."

"Random variables be like: I don't know what I am. Meanwhile confident chad Gaussian distributions be like: if it wasn't for me being responsible for the central limit theorem, you peasants would have no complexity and only entropy."

The ones with strange sounds are among the best. Despite farts as a facet of humor being used in jokes in the 21st century, for some reason, variations of this sound simply did not seem to go away. Even today, a random fart here or there can breathe life into a boring joke that fell flat on its face. Then there are the ones that are completely inhuman. Beeps synchronized to sorting algorithms, squeaky noises whenever a supernova could be seen in the distance back when they still happened, a snoring black hole. While many of these are quite bizarre, they still have something about them that appear to be somewhat relatable to a human. I suppose that is what makes them humorous. There is something to ground them within my mind. The best jokes seem to be the ones that are meta and complex with self-references and high level connections between ideas and concepts that have nothing to do with each other on a surface level. Such inside jokes can make mundane, everyday things humorous because they implicate something deeper that is the source of the joke. Similar to hearing a random default Android notification out of the blue, the simple parts of everyday life have transformed into the centerpieces of jokes that are difficult to explain, but do not seem to lose their freshness. Over the years, while the jokes become more and more unrecognizable to the humans of the past, they still manage to tie in some aspect of the universe around us. Although we have been running out of material as everything gradually went dark, humor, which has been one of the only coping mechanisms we had left, never went away. Even now, we find a way around the obstacles placed in front of us by diving deep into our memories and transforming them into their many permutations like a machine learning algorithm training itself on the same data over and over again and increasing its training data through clever mathematical tricks. Our humor no longer draws from what has happened, but also what is possible, what is impossible, and everything in between.

Of course, when it comes to memes and jokes, part of the appeal is being able to share them with others. To enjoy such an experience, we have effectively created a social network of one person: me. It is not so much an interconnected web, but rather a common space that can be visited by any part of myself as we please. We created a user interface within our imagination, not unlike the social networks of the past, where we can generate profiles which represent the parts of us we want to show to others. It is a superficial gesture seeing as we are all one person and we know fully well what each other is thinking. Despite this, we consciously participate in this charade, to wring out whatever joy we can by carrying out this exercise. We construct multiple chat rooms and forums within a multiverse in which we can interact with each other and share the jokes we have. We have back and forth conversations where we try to outdo what was previously posted. One image gets downloaded, photoshopped, and then re-uploaded to try to improve upon what came before. Before long, we have forgotten what the original looked like and all our attention is focused on the surreal creation that shows as most recent in our message thread. These conversations I have with myself initially felt like a futile struggle against my loneliness, but eventually these different parts of my personality and my identity that I split myself into seemed to almost take on the appearance and presence of separate individuals with minds of their own.

Somewhere along the line, I was no longer playing a role, but was instead looking in a fractured mirror where each reflection seemed to have its own opinions and takes on different topics. I could bounce ideas off of each one, watch them talk to each other, and see them develop over time. Each one had their own ego with their own distinct idiosyncrasies. Sometimes, they would pick up habits and ideas from others and co-opt them, becoming similar, or growing. The interactions were soon taken out of the social networks and became more complex. Anything that people could do with each other, we did with one another: music, art, love, conflict, all of it.

Music and art in particular were very interesting and followed a trajectory similar to our sense of humor. In the case of musical improvisation in a group, while we began with traditional instruments and sounds, once we realized that the limitations we had previously no longer applied, our sounds and melodies entered the realm of the otherworldly. It is not simply a matter of playing the right notes. Eventually, it grows in complexity. Soon, it is quick repeatable patterns of key changes. Later, it became a matter of changing the instrument that plays a particular part in the middle of a bar. Nothing is off limits, which means that anything can happen regardless of whether it is physically possible or not. As long as it has a certain level of predictability, then it is still musical. If it can be followed, then it is music. This seems to be the nuance between sounds with musical qualities, and pure noise. One has recognizable patterns while the other does not. The pattern does not necessarily need to be easy to follow, but it needs to be there. That is the basic requirement. Outside of that, anything can happen. Replace your musical instruments with the whirs and hums of machinery, remove a part completely, use silence as a central part of your song. The structure of songs themselves can also be completely unconventional where they do not necessarily have a beginning or an end, but transition from one part to another in a loop like an auditory Möbius strip that ends where it begins and begins where it ends. Conversely, they can become inverted where melodies become the backing while the backing takes center stage. Some of these concepts have been tried in 21st century music, but others such as the infinite loop are not as conventional. Then there are the vocals. In this world, to overcome the limitations of the human voice, there is more than just autotune. Voices can be modulated and changed without limit. Sometimes, the human aspects can be merged with other instruments or the sounds of other animals to create something alien. Language too is without limitation. Instead of sticking to a single language, words from different parts of the globe as well as languages that never existed can be used to form sentences and verses regardless of grammatical coherence. For us, there is no need for language other than to organize our thoughts as one being, so language can take on a more abstract form to suit our artistic needs. A little bit of Mandarin here, some Arabic here, and let's sprinkle in some ancient Greek to spice things up. It doesn't matter if it makes sense. In fact that is better. The harder it is to make connections between the words, the more the listener has to work to make the music work for them. It is an exercise in self-gratification through forcing a certain level of imagination and creativity on the listener.

Film is no exception either. In addition to the sequels, there are also original movie premises playing rent free in our head. Can you imagine that the Rocky franchise has made it all the way to 5000 sequels? I can't either. At first, watching Rocky go back in time to box Hitler was thought to be the peak. However, soon we kept topping the previous entry until we hit 5000. There's something that never gets old about overcoming adversity to eventually triumph. I tried to hold a Rocky marathon, but somewhere along the line, I forgot the plot events for a large amount of them which shortened the marathon significantly. Rocky is no exception. George Lucas would be rolling in his grave if he saw what we did with Star Wars. Disney would likely be collecting trillions and quadrillions of royalties from other properties. All those oversaturated superhero movies just keep coming and coming regardless of whether they are good or bad. What is nice about the current creative environment is that we are no longer motivated by the box office, subscribers to a streaming service or a financial quarter, so anything is allowed. We can make every indie film and every indie film with too large of a budget. It all lives in our head, so there are no costs or liabilities borne in terms of special effects, computer graphics or stunt work. Some of the actors who form a part of me need some way to pass the time, so we can create works that not only have an unlimited budget with perfect visuals, but also add in the star power and recognition that the films of old had. It is the best of both worlds when we can keep a stable mind. There are those among us who saw this as an opportunity to create a virtual currency based on an economy of thoughts and ideas, but that was quickly shot down as idiotic and as a way to pointlessly impose limits on ourselves. When anything is possible, why introduce currencies and scarcity when it serves no purpose?

"Don't ruin it. We did enough of that before."

In addition to the stars and celebrities that were alive at the time of the curse, there are the stars and celebrities that were born out here in space through the amalgamation of the best qualities of some of the more admirable individuals within the industry. Some of them were not even human. Finally, the dead have been brought back to life to cameo in the summer blockbusters. Imagine Marlon Brando or Laurence Olivier making powerful appearances on the scene and reminding everyone of what acting is. It is an everlasting golden age of ideas and creativity. The number of high quality items outputted varies from time to time, but it has its ups and downs. You never know when inspiration strikes, or when parts of you become too mentally exhausted to play along. The lulls in creative output have made it hard to pass the time, but it also allowed for a break in the frantic output in an attempt to forget about the situation we have been forced into.

With the dying universe and our limited ability to observe the world around us, our reasoning and imagination has been strengthened tremendously. This has enabled us to effectively live in worlds of our own creation without a need to care about what is happening on the outside. The inside has become all that mattered and it is the mechanism by which we can live a semblance of a life. The many lives we have experienced have been countless and have taken place on planets, in space, in impossible locations, and in realities with their own unique rules. There have been realities with magic, fantastical places with superheroes and realities where we can live completely unencumbered by time, space, and any limitations other than the ones that accompany our mental processes. Imagination and thought have effectively been the tools that we used to seek solace from the chains that bound us in the real world. At times there are some nagging thoughts that can break the dream.

"None of this is real."

"We still suffer within our dreams."

The human condition is one of ups and downs and as a result, we experience traumatic events within our dreams that remind us of painful times. At the same time, overexposure to happy moments and a continuous deluge of wish fulfillment have dulled our senses to the point that the ups no longer feel like the good times and seem more like business as normal. What is good is boring, and what is bad can stand out when you place your hands over your non-existent ears and try to close your non-existent eyes.

The dreams that were the most painful were the ones that took place here in the present. Not in the past when we were humans and not in another world where we can escape, but here in our present where we are facing against a doomed future. The dreams that took place in our present that gave us hope or introduced change into an unchanging environment were the ones that made us feel something again. In one such episode where we were dreaming while awake, I imagined that one of those friends, those companions that traveled alongside me throughout the early part of my existence, came back. They came back all grown up and capable of understanding who we are. They came back, hardened by the pressures of this dying universe, and reached a point where nothing can threaten their existence anymore. While they could have left and never visited us again, they came back. They came back to this grotesque creature who could not speak or provide. They came back despite the challenge of doing so and with no expectation of payment or reward. They had no physical presence, but for our sake, they took on a form that allowed for us to see them as though they were another entity we could interact it. In our time of solitary confinement in the largest prison, they knocked on the bars to our cell in the form of a winged ball of light and said, "Hello."

The visions I had were of one of a great dialogue that lasted for thousands of years of greetings where we made each other's acquaintance and grew to know one another as different civilizations. It initially began as a series of signals, like a light based Morse code. This eventually changed to a number of tests where they streamed different types of particles towards us to see what effect it had. Eventually, they managed to transmit sound directly within our minds and we could communicate through a sort of telepathic means. At first, the conversations were crude as they gradually compiled a vocabulary and grammars and as we tried to adhere to a single language. What was originally a number of questions regarding names, time, and location eventually became more full-fledged conversations with more abstract details. They told us of their story and their beginnings as a civilization. They explained where their home planet was and the trajectory of their growth as a people. We learned that they were not just one species, but a coalition of many species that evolved from similar species on a planet located many lightyears away from where Earth once was. We told them of our history. How we grew and multiplied, how we left the pull of our planet, created artificial intelligence, and how we found ourselves like this. They attempted to explain to us the mechanisms of how they were able to establish communication while we tried to build upon our understanding of physics to reach some level of comprehension of what exactly we have become. Their descriptions of unconventional states of matter and nested loops of time would fly over our head. We discussed cultural similarities and how the way we think was dependent upon our physical states and the languages we use to describe our environment. There were times when nuances were lost, or when single words would have multiple meanings which resulted in ambiguities when discussing complex ideas. It is one thing to make a simple greeting in another language, it is another to have a fluid conversation, and it is another to discuss highly specialized topics within that language. These frustrations were gradually smoothed out over the years, but when such situations did appear, we found ourselves explaining simple concepts in a highly detailed manner, or reverting to using mathematics to find common ground. As math can be fairly unambiguous and precise, it was a good method by which to eliminate situations where clarity may be lacking. With that said, the act of using math as a medium by which to communicate certain things can be draining. While they have computational capabilities that are orders of magnitude more advanced than anything we have ever developed prior to the curse, we simply have a human level intelligence with the memories of billions of humans. When it came to such conversations, we were undoubtedly the bottleneck and I remember being quite grateful with how patient they were during such exchanges. It is not an understatement when I state that our technological achievements and the knowledge we gained over the years were nothing in the face of a civilization that managed to survive up to this point and freely travel through the universe as though they were taking a languid stroll through the countryside.

We eventually arrived upon what was to become of us. We could simply vanish into the darkness. However, they told me that to do so would be a waste of an opportunity. They told us of a place where we could live. Not in another time or in another universe, but in this same universe. We were told that there were many faces to this reality, and what we knew was but a fragment of what was out there. We were supposedly just fish living within a glass of water that gradually gained cracks over time, and that there was an ocean out there. It was far away, but it was out there. There, we could live if we so pleased. We could have a place to call our own, a return to the individual identities and bodies we once had, and an appropriate amount of guidance to ensure that we do not repeat the mistakes of the past. The stories they told of these hidden parts of the universe were fantastical. There were monsters and giants out there of which they knew, and they believed that there were deities and gods surpassing even them in the spaces beyond which they have yet to comprehend. They told us of creatures that traveled from universe to universe, imparting wisdom to intelligent species or poaching them by introducing varying amounts of entropy into closed systems. They told us of battles being fought between conservationists and prospectors hoping to either preserve or exploit multidimensional reserves. There were battles and wars that transcended time, space, dimensions, probability, and even mathematics and common logic. These are metaphysical wars that are beyond the comprehension of our companion, but they have enough capacity to at least understand such battles were occurring. Within such a tapestry of interplay, we were to live within a small portion of a multiversal reserve that was being protected by the environmentalists on the outside of our three dimensional fishbowl.

At the same time, they offered us three other choices. The first was to take us into the past and place us where we once stood. All the problems and luxuries we had would once more be ours to carry if we choose, and we would be able to live out the fate we would have lived if there had been no interference whatsoever. The second was to offer each and every one of us a life that suited our tastes. All of us would go on to live a life of our choosing in different parallel universes. It was a tempting offer. Finally, the third choice was to simply leave us alone to see our current state through to the end wherever or whenever it may be. They would simply leave, and nothing would happen. In the case of the first two, we were also given the option of keeping our memories of this ordeal we have spent the lifetime of the universe experiencing, or erasing them and reverting to zero.

Each possibility had its appeal and its own set of

disadvantages, some more than others. By the time we made a decision, the dream stopped. I don't think any of us wanted to know what we chose, since doing so may reveal more of ourselves than we wished to know. In the case we did make a decision, knowing of the unchangeable aftermath may also be soul crushing. It is strange how despite being a species that desires change, we are also afraid of it. We only want to improve our situation, but rarely do we wish to take risks to that end which may also result in setbacks. Of course, there is always the risk of inaction which, while it may result from indecision, is a decision in and of itself.

There was one other dream that I found deeply unsettling. It was one where we found ourselves face to face with the one who placed us in this situation. When given the chance to converse, to ask questions, to plead and beg, we stayed silent. Here was the one who holds our fate in its hands, and yet we are unable to do anything. It was not because we were incapable of action, of thought, or speech, but rather because we chose not to act. The being that made us this way chose to take on a form that we would understand and sense. It would place itself right in front of us, and wait. It does not ask anything of us or act. It just stays there, and in the face of inaction, we are unable to do anything. What happens to us is completely up to us, but we do not think a thought, demand an answer, throw an insult, or react in fear.

We defined ourselves by what we did. Our accomplishments were the sum of our actions. However, in the time when it mattered the most, we did nothing, and the dream ended. In the place of those visions were nothing more than voices echoing back at us. They tell us of the mistakes we have made, the mistakes we are making, and the mistakes that we will make. All we can do in response is to simply dream another dream and hope for a satisfying ending.

CHAPTER 17: STEPS TOWARDS THE FINISH LINE

The birth was difficult. Before the predicted due date, her body was already weak and it was uncertain what medical complications might arise during the final days of the pregnancy. We think we can depend on modern medicine, but it is just a stop gap for the creeping fate that all of us have. This is assuming that proper treatment is provided which is not always the case when considering all of the bureaucratic hoops the average patient needs to jump through in addition to placing oneself at the mercy of human error. Childbirth is always traumatic to the body regardless of the level of health of the mother, and it leaves its mark and shortens the lifespan. Such is the price of creating another life. It is the price that accompanies carrying a child for nine months. It is a price that is paid in the form of effectively running the human body at a higher speed and under a higher load so that it can properly account for the life that it will eventually bring into the world. Heart rate, metabolism, blood pressure, hormones... all are affected. In such conditions, one has to wonder what is prioritized by evolution: the life of the mother, or the life of the child? One has the potential to produce more offspring and raise the offspring while the other is the future of the species. For some species, birth kills the mother while producing multiple offspring while for others, offspring are plentiful to the point where cannibalism is sometimes not only not counterproductive, but also encouraged depending on the situation. For us humans, however, the child seems to serve greater importance.

In a sense, the moment one's offspring is born, it becomes the beginning of the end. You as a person die, and in its place is a drone that serves the needs of the child. Your hopes and dreams become lowered in priority, and whatever you may have had planned are less valid. To intentionally have a child is very much an act of self-sacrifice as it is a shifting of priorities. You effectively push your hopes and dreams onto your child because time is running out for you. This, in a sense, is also a way of holding back one's descendants. You missed your chance, so you leave everything to the next generation, sometimes forcing your ideals on your children to negative effect. It is something humans in every era have been guilty of. Your accomplishments are only relevant to the present and forcing them upon the next generation is proof of living in the past. It is as though an ape is telling a human to climb a tree instead of walking on two feet. It is as though a knight is admonishing an office worker for being unable to duel to the death. It is a form of generational procrastination where the previous generation imposes their will on the next while also diminishing their will in the present. Your child is a message in a bottle to the future. In the process, you not only give yourself for the sake of the child, but also acknowledge that you have become a lost cause. The future is no longer about you. Furthermore, the future that you are in the process of building is not one you will ever see or fully understand. That future has no place for you. You are old news, and if you raise your child well enough, you may be able to redeem yourself and your failures. You do this because your legacy is the only thing that we believe truly lasts. The tree that dies is replaced by the forest it seeds. That is the idea. From your efforts, a lineage that will eventually make a dent will emerge and validate your efforts. Of course, the cycle never stops. Your children will attempt to succeed and by failing in doing so, they push their plans onto their children as well. Humanity is nothing more than a series of failures where any sense of progress is truly gained by learning from the past. When the mistakes of the past no longer apply, new types of challenges and the respective failures that originate from them make an appearance. It is not simply that we are always failing, but rather that we are usually failing at different things.

The first steps were a memorable moment. It was definitely strange to see a creature completely incapable of caring for itself move with autonomy and intention. Stubby limbs and uncoordinated movements eventually result in the convergence of controlled actions. The very idea was a paradox. These first steps were not only an exercise in moving the body, but to move it with a certain level of confidence and conviction. The act of walking is difficult for robots to replicate, but this child could do it so effortlessly and only improved over time. Although we take this for granted, the act of walking and navigating through a space is actually complex. Walking is something we do every day, but for our child, the first time was a milestone for hundreds of millions of steps to follow. This is the beginning of a journey that starts at a road that extends far beyond the horizon. From the perspective of a parent, it was an exciting moment, but also one of concern, because the ability to move forward could be a double edged sword. On one hand, the only way we progress is by putting one step in front of the other by moving in an incremental manner. Conversely, if you are not looking, you could easily walk your way off a cliff simply because you are unaware of what to watch out for. I suppose that is where my responsibilities lie: to ensure that our future progresses in the right direction. What is the right direction? No one knows. If you are an incompetent parent, the *right* direction is simply any direction away from you. It is any direction that can reduce your responsibility and workload. How I wish I could run away from this responsibility without any regrets. However, my obligations seem to guilt me into staying where I am despite it not necessarily being in my best interests.

I hope I am not an incompetent parent, but I cannot predict the future. A family is a relationship of mutual trust. Whether that trust becomes broken or not requires the cooperation of all parties. I hope that this child will grow in a stable household and I will act in a manner to ensure that that becomes a reality. However, I am well aware that effort is merely a prerequisite for results. At the end of the day, luck and outside conditions play a significant role.

Of course, at some point, this child will need some form of independence and a family is just a foundation that acts as bedrock to take flight from. I hope that he will be able to realize that although life can be carried out alone, to be human requires participation in society and interaction with others from the day of birth. Although I hope our descendants can transcend society, our biology prevents us from doing so. When the time comes, will he be able to make friends? Will our child have the capabilities needed to find allies in the many wars each and every one of us inevitably fights so as to live and live well? In the battle against time and expedition to progress through life, will he be able to navigate the challenges and claim victory? All we can do is simply provide our children with the tools needed to handle the world. Whether they use them or not and how they use those tools, skills, and experiences is ultimately within their hands. The responsibility that weighs us down as parents early in a child's growth can weigh us down even later in life when we have little control. The guilt and obligation can act as a curse or a burden even though it does not feel wrong to wish to have some level of influence on factors we ultimately have no rights to control. Our child too is an individual with their own thoughts and emotions. As parents, what we can do is be there and guide them.

As we consider the future, our own thoughts about our relationships become uncertain. We do not know what will happen to us. Will we be there to watch this child grow? To have such a privilege cannot be taken for granted. Similarly, we do not know if these relationships will always exist. Will we fight? What will we fight over? Will it be something trivial that ends it all, or will it be a number of mistakes and failures cascading until something gives and breaks the camel's back? Yes, relationships do not last forever. However, they are best when they are positive. The nature of the universe is one of increasing entropy. To maintain order, energy is required to keep the forces of chaos at bay. I do not wish for us to become estranged. I do not wish to grow old while they never think of me. I do not want to be hated for years on end while constantly thinking of how I can gain forgiveness. That is a life I do not want to live. I do not want to live without a family. I do not want to live without people I can trust. In my old age, will they be there for me? Will they care for me when I can no longer care for myself?

I can envision myself at the end of all of this dying alone as I know many others have. I can see the same fate befall my spouse, our child, his children, and many others. I can see the earth rotting to dust long and combusting within the sun after our graves have been defiled by nature and there is nothing to remember us by. I can see us being remembered by our children and perhaps grandchildren and then being forgotten by our descendants afterwards with nothing more than a gravestone to stand as some proof that we have lived. I can see the same happening to our children as well. Unless you are a great leader, a conqueror, a mass murderer, or an influential thinker, you simply do not matter. Those closest to you will be the last ones to remember you, and as time passes, you will be lost to the sands of time. No one will remember you. No one will know you existed. You will have died never leaving a mark, and even if you did, you will be outshined by those who came before you and left a larger mark. Even they will no longer matter when the last human dies, when our culture vanishes, and when the earth turns to ash. Nothing is permanent including you and the marks you and your descendants tried to leave.

CHAPTER 18: PROGENY

It's too late for us now. And it is too far for anyone to follow. There is a regret that I could not use my knowledge and insights gained through this ordeal to help others. To warn others not to follow in our steps. To tell those who come after to savor life while it lasts and how to train themselves to endure hardship. It is too late for any of that. There is no one to convey these things to, and there never will be. The lessons I learned are for me and me alone. Whomever still exists in this universe will cease to exist, and new life is gradually becoming an impossibility. The family of intelligent life is an endangered group, and though I may wish to not be alone, this wish will never come to fruition. Be it through our cosmic neighbors or through descendants, life as we know it will no longer originate within this cold space.

"What's done is done. No use worrying about a future that will never occur."

Our wish to have a legacy that outlives us is also buried. We cannot have any children or anything resembling offspring. We cannot pass our teachings onto anyone, and there are many among us that think that is for the best. Our presence may be a corrupting force rather than one for good. Our universe is a putrid carcass. Our friends are lost within the infinity. Why would I want to bring anything into this dying universe when all it is going to do is starve and wither away? If life is suffering, then I would simply be continuing the cycle. There is no Garden of Eden. We cannot be fruitful and multiply. There is no plentiful bounty provided to us by nature. We cannot fill this reality and subdue it. We cannot subdue it, raze it to the ground and pass barren land to our offspring like our forebears did. That time has passed. There is nothing left for those who follow but existential pain. To bring life into such conditions is simply cruelty. We know of what pain is in store. If we do not wish to experience it, why would our children?

"Common sense seems to trump tradition. Our duty brought upon us by cultural and societal norms are irrelevant in conditions where cause and effect are seemingly absent."

Indeed, I wonder if our predecessors thought the same thing. Did our parents think of the destruction and misery they would be imposing upon their children, or did they naively believe that their actions were responsible and just? Truly, we stood on the shoulders of cannibalistic vampires. Did they even think of how we would denounce their actions as barbaric and thoughtless? It is questionable whether they thought at all. It feels as though human attention is much like that of human vision: that which is on the periphery has minimal importance. Those who are close are the ones who matter, and the strangers of the world are worthless. "My child will grow to be successful, and your children are of no concern. In fact, your children are competition that should be eliminated as soon as possible." We are creatures of ego toeing the line between selfishness and altruism. Sometimes altruism wins out, but usually the desires of the individual takes priority. This is particularly the case among those with low levels of self-control, empathy, long term planning or some combination of the three. This is not without reason. Our experience is ours alone. The pain of others is not ours to feel. The challenges that we face as individuals are the most immediate and pressing. Our life is the only one we experience and our death is the one that ends it all.

It is because of this that we are driven by our personal desires for the majority of our lives. This means that all of us knows what it means to never follow our dreams, to suffer in agony, and to wallow in disappointment. We all know what the ups and downs are, and we are well aware that it is our death which ends everything and takes away all that ails us and all that gives us joy. In the end, we are in a constant state of deprivation.

That is what life is. Anything you gain will be lost in the end. The question is whether that loss is worth the life you lived. There is much disagreement on this matter. In the past, I used to wish I was dead. Now, I wish I had never been born.

"To never know is to look forward to a limitless future. Ignorance can have the illusion of freedom with the benefits of obliviousness to all the pain."

The decision to live is not a decision that we make. It is made for us. It is made for us without our consent. Whether you are born into riches or born into slavery, your life is not something that you chose. In many cases, who you become and who you can become has been decided by a series of events that came into play long before you were capable of conscious thought. Life, in other words, is forced upon us and the death that follows is forced upon us as well. For the unborn, it could be said that they are the lucky ones for they never will experience death. They will never endure hardship, they will never know what it is to gain everything you wanted to only lose it all in the end. Life is a zero sum gain. You can bring your hopes up. You can think of those you love, the things you leave behind and use that to justify its worth. However, all those things are as impermanent as you. They too will not last. They too will be forgotten.

It feels strange to say it, but life seems so unnatural despite it being of natural origins. We all feel that we are meant for something more, but it is truth that we were all originally born only to die. We were never meant to be the final product. We were solely a footnote in a series of footnotes. It begs the question of what is the final product if it is not us. If we are only a part of the process, then that means that we were never meant to be the final product. It is as though we are a means to an end that we do not have the capacity to understand or predict. We are the tree that is to be chopped down to become lumber. Eventually that lumber will serve a purpose in the construction of other objects, but the tree will never live to see what it becomes no matter how beautiful and ornate that destiny may be. Life is a means to an end. That end is one we were meant to be around to see. Our life is merely a process that creates byproducts that can later be used by others. Nothing more, nothing less. Your life may be yours while you live it, but only then. It is nothing before and nothing after. That is not to say that it is not important. However, it is only as important as a hammer is to a carpenter or a supply chain is to an industry. It is the machine that builds what is truly needed. Just as the stars were for us, it is likely that we were the same for whatever it is that comes next. What may be, is difficult to tell in this void that permeates all of existence.

Knowing that we will never know what comes after, what it is we were meant to create is one of those truths that eats away at oneself like acid on rock. The knowledge and reason that we torment ourselves with is not enough to provide us with all the answers. Though we know this now, I wonder if those who brought us into this world knew as well and still did so despite knowing. There is a deep resentment for those who brought us into this life which never ends. They lived in peace, experiencing their pain for a finite period of time while I am here to rage against the shadows. I resent myself for bringing life into the world as well. To see my own children suffer the same fate that I am makes me wish that I had never created life if this was in store. There is no need for others to share the same fate and yet I, through my ignorance, selfishly brought this punishment upon them.

Lo and behold: here too do I repeat the mistakes of those who came before me despite I myself being a victim of their actions. If we were never cursed, would we too have cannibalized our young as our ancestors did? Would we too act as a drain on the youth of our successors as they march towards death by following in our footsteps? I wonder if our current form is not much different from the form we once had. We were already cursed before. This state of being did not change that. If we were to have children through some miracle, it may indeed be true that we would betray them as our predecessors betrayed us by forcefully imposing life upon them. Life and death is the curse and nirvana is out of our reach. To never experience either is to experience true freedom through ignorance. At least then do we never experience our hopes and dreams being trampled by reality and ending in our passing which ultimately signifies nothing and leaves a fading legacy that too passes into insignificance with the march of time.

PART 4

A Whimper

CHAPTER 19: THE DARK ERA

After the passing of over googol years, we are finally witness to the Dark Era. Turn back. There is nothing here and no hope of reprieve. There is nothing to be gained by continuing on this path. After an infinite amount of time, only zero is left. It's all a dead end. Nothing happens on a human time scale. Nothing happens on a cosmic time scale. Nothing happens. There are no victories, only losses. It is a waiting game of seeing if anything occurs to minimal avail. This is not only true on the large-scale, but also on the quantum scale. Particles are beginning to break down and antiparticles occasionally make an appearance to annihilate their counterparts. Entropy in this system has reached a point where complexity and computation have become near impossible. By extension, thought and sentience supported by standard matter also becomes impossible. For anything to be born in this sealed tomb of a universe, it must come from a side of it that we do not yet fully grasp. For those who were looking for a way out, the door is shut and locked from the other side. The only way out now is to reverse the clock. If there are other options, it is beyond our intellect. The game is over. The quiet requiem heard throughout the universe has now become sheet music filled with rests. There are half rests, quarter rests, whole rests, but rests nonetheless. The song is still playing. You just can't hear it.

CHAPTER 20: A PALE HORSE

I had once presumed I was some kind of invincible ghost unaffected by what occurs around me, but it seems as though that is not the case. There have been changes. Whether these changes are caused by the nature of the universe or the nature of my situation is questionable. What is becoming apparent is that my mind and its mental faculties are deteriorating. Simple thoughts become a chore and every act of mental labor has grown slower and slower. I can feel myself becoming stretched out over time. I no longer know if a thought takes nanoseconds, seconds, or years. Of course, it does not make a difference anymore, but there are gaps in the chain of ideas and feelings that I travel along. My memory is starting to degenerate into Swiss cheese, and I cannot do anything to reverse the onset of this mental degradation. To fight against it is like swimming against a raging current. We keep forgetting, and coherent thoughts are becoming fewer and fewer. If I could choose the memories that I lose, it may be acceptable, but the loss of my grip on the past is indiscriminate. It is irrelevant how important a memory may be, I can still lose it. My mind is gradually being torn from me. The things we used to identify ourselves and understand who we are incrementally disappearing. Life now is a mixture of thoughts and memories I don't wish to experience, and thoughts and memories that I will never experience again. We too are becoming a void, and the gradual decay of our mentality signifies that at some point that we will be incapable of thought. What this means is that the only thing that I can still use to convince myself that I exist will be gone. Will it be individual parts of me that drop off like flies, or will it be a memory of a person here and thought from another person here? Will I cease to remember that I am the entirety of a species, or will I begin to believe that I am one human separated from the rest? What will I be at the end of this? I don't know, but the closest thing to the loss of all thought that I am aware of is brain death. There will be no more conscious thought and the absence of reason. As much as I believed it impossible, death is coming for us, and this time, I don't think that there is anything to stop it.

Although I wish to rage against death, there is nothing I can do, and no one left here to save me. It is now that I realize what death is, and that frightens me deeply. When death comes, I will not realize it. We realize that we are to die and what that means on our deathbed. However, the truth is that we were already on our deathbed. We just didn't notice yet. By the time I am dead, I will be devoid of thought and unable to comprehend whether I am living or not. Anything I wanted to do, any thought I want to have will be impossible. I will be unable to see what comes after or know what effect my death has had. Perhaps there may be an afterlife, and that could have some comfort, but if an afterlife is merely an extension of life, then all of the problems I have experienced during life will be present there as well. I wonder if an afterlife is merely nothing more than a way to calm the hearts of cowards who are unable to realize and comprehend what death is. In one moment, I have autonomy and identity. In the next, everything is taken away from me. We become nothing. We become something that is no longer us, and when it happens, we won't know. If we were still human, perhaps we may be given a grave. However, we will be dead, and a grave means nothing to the dead. For us who will be unable to appreciate it, it will only hold value for the living and nothing else.

We have seen the deaths of many, but our own is the one that has significance. It is the one that directly affects us. Other deaths may cause sadness, but those are footnotes on our journey to the end. Like roadkill littering the streets, we did not have a second thought of those who passed away once we moved on. The corpse left behind is only there as a reminder, but it means less to us than the living being that inhabited it. Once a body is torn to shreds, mutilated, beheaded, burnt to a crisp, and becomes unrecognizable, its meaning fundamentally changes. Open casket, closed casket, missing or cremated—no one is home. The more I ponder the physical nature of death, the more alien the human body seems to me. There is no reason why our worth and our ideation should be dependent upon the physical nature of our existence and yet we cannot imagine ourselves without it. We can't think of ourselves as anything else other than a collection of arms, legs, eyes, and meat, but we never think of the individual parts. All of it is us, and all of it affects how we think.

When we turn off a machine, we do not consider it to be dead. However, when a human becomes brain dead, that human is. If a machine is broken, if its data can be transferred to another body, it can be born anew. Perhaps human life is identical and we simply need to rerun our source code to wake up from death like a robot may wake up when its batteries are recharged and it is turned back on. If given an infinite amount of time, could it be possible that we can be reborn through completely random processes like a work of Shakespeare born from typewriters operated by monkeys with no time limit? Maybe there are many people who are waiting to be reborn in a new form that transcends the biological and physical substrate we are so familiar with. We could instead be reborn as creatures whose thoughts travel across the universe at the speed of light on the back of subatomic particles. It is wishful thinking, but among the many promises of an afterlife, it is also not the most unreasonable.

This reflection on what death may be has led me to admire those who were able to live while risking death and those who truly understood what death was, but were able to give up their lives in self-sacrifice regardless. I have often asked, what is worse: living afraid of death, living unafraid of death, not living at all despite being alive, or to never live at all. To not live despite being living is obviously worse than many of the other possibilities. It is regretful to not make the best of life while you have it. However, what of the other possibilities? To be afraid of death could indeed be counterproductive, but if one is not aware of death, one cannot value life. This provides a quandary where one must accept a certain level of risk to live their life to the fullest while minimizing risk so that such a life is not cut too short. There is a balance there that I have not appreciated in the past for good reason. If a person were to contemplate their death every waking moment, nothing can happen. I do not think that we humans, despite our intelligence, have evolved to do such a thing. On an individual scale, death is always in the background. It is rarely front and center on our list of concerns. An afterlife can be a crutch to overcome such fears, but it can be a distraction as well. There has been no shortage of stupidity that has used an afterlife to justify acts which contained a chance of death. It is one thing to not fear death while living for the promise of an afterlife. It is another to not fear death while living with no guarantee of an afterlife. I do not know where people can find the courage to overcome such fears, but for those who have faced death and lived, they have believed that there are things worth risking life for. Be it family, country, friends, or the greater good, there was something which became the crowning jewel of a life well lived to justify the sacrifice. What that is for us, I do not know. In a reality where none of those things exist anymore, there is nothing to make us rush bravely into death as we have once done.

It is here that I recognize that life has never truly been important in the grand scheme of things. It is of value to me. However, that is only because I am alive. Is it of value to the dead or the unborn? I'm not so sure about that. It is important to those who benefit from me being alive. Not too surprisingly, those individuals are alive as well. So, it stands to reason that life is only of value for the living. What that value is, is questionable. I feel like life should not be quantified in dollars and currency, but the past suggests that it clearly can. Each organ has its own value. Be it in the black market, or in health care, every procedure has a price tag. If you add the value of all the parts of the human body, do you arrive at the value of a human? I don't think so, but I think that a human is more than the sum of their parts. They are also the sum of their actions. What it is that a person does during their life and what they are capable of is also of value. If not, how would workplaces have ultimately decided who to hire and who to lay off? Obviously, there is a comparison of values and traits. The slave trade which continued in some form from the birth of civilization to modern times also tried to place a price on individuals. However, it was a very crude form of measurement due to the fact that a slave's potential was never considered nor fulfilled. A slave is cheap labor. What they were capable of was of no interest to their owners.

If we were to apply the concepts of scarcity and supply and demand, then the question of whether humans were more valuable in the past compared to today arises. At times when humans were fewer, they could be said to be more valuable. However, one aspect of this value is missed and that is the temporal aspect. As time passes, the effect one can have on the future decreases as well. It is easier to have a greater influence on the future of civilization when civilization was just beginning to form. Were those humans worth more? In modern times when the human population was high, there was more where that came from. However, now, in this moment, it seems like a commodity that can never exist ever again. Perhaps it is within that scarcity that it has value. However, there is only value when there is demand. As everyone dies off, demand dies off with it. Simply put, the dead are incapable of desiring life, and in this realm of nothing, once I am gone, there will be no one alive to wish to stay alive. Do we have a duty as the last of our kind to remember those who came before us? I don't know. Should we not remember them so that they do not die a second death? Or is that simply entrapment? Would we instead have been made prisoners of the dead who no longer concern themselves with

143

the living? It is likely. If the dead could speak, would they say anything differently that what we already have? I think not.

Life is a selfish existence that desires itself. Once it is gone, nothing will desire it ever again.

CHAPTER 21: AN UNFULFILLED PURPOSE

The moment you dwell on former triumphs is the instant you admit the past is behind you. That realization struck us mere decades after becoming like this. The years that followed rubbed salt in the wound. There is always that gnawing, nagging thought that we could have been much more. Much more than this at least. The thought has nothing to back it up, but it leads to a question of what I could have been. For those of us who were successful, we could have continued in that manner, collecting victory after victory. For some of us, we could have experienced a fall from grace while those who were hungry for a better life could have toppled the standing of those at the top. As much as it pains us to say, modern society was nothing more than a series of trading places, a revolving door of roles along some form of hierarchy in the hopes that one day you can call it quits. But that is just the short term. That is just the timescale of a human life. That's peanuts compared to what humanity could have accomplished.

Where we left off, our environment was being ravaged at the hands of our industry while we inflicted pain on each other to maintain some vain semblance of control over the status quo. We created the conditions that necessitated charity while chastising those who were not charitable. We set fire to our biosphere despite the advantages it provided us, and deemed doing so as "good". If we did not change course, we may have been able to witness the fall of governments and restructuring of the world order. Would we have become completely extinct? It is questionable. I believe that while our foolishness was capable of decimating the human population, it was not quite at the level that we could be wiped out completely. Sapiens have been likened to viruses which spread indiscriminately in the past. Extinction is unlikely unless there were sudden changes in the environment that were incomparable to trends seen in the past. The Earth, despite its changing nature, would still be habitable, and we were fully capable of surviving on other planets. In times of desperation, it is completely feasible for us to survive. Yet, who survives is another matter entirely. Rather, it is a question of who is important or lucky enough to survive. I imagine the ugly fights that occur in such situations would remind us of some of the darkest moments in human history. Any time we choose who lives and who dies, the worst seems to come out in people. If that was to be our legacy, then perhaps we have been given a boon.

Nevertheless, there are parts of me that think that humanity is ultimately good. They believe that those who wish the best for us as a whole will rise to the top and eventually form the majority of the ruling class without being corrupted in any form. These individuals would supposedly transcend the endless pursuit for more. While it is certainly not impossible, many of us consider such thinking to be naïve. Even so, escapism is our only respite now, so we entertain the thought. Why not? What form would humanity take if it managed to pull together and straighten itself out? What would we have become if the systems that we operated within were not corroded at their very foundations? How would the seeds we planted take root to give birth to a lush forest? The standard utopian visions are the first to be proposed and then struck down. We know what human nature is like. Whatever form human civilization takes will either find a way to remove the flaws of human nature, or incorporate it into its structure. Which is easier? Do we have the capacity to find a system that works for us, or will we brute force the problem by using technology to surveil our behavior at granular levels and engineer ourselves to no longer have impure thoughts and imperfections? Both sound incredibly complex. The former requires a set of laws that can grow and change quickly enough to accommodate the changing interests of humans. The latter requires determining what precursors can lead to damaging outcomes and stopping those in their tracks. Both require a certain level of foresight. Will we still be allowed to feel certain emotions? Can we still think certain thoughts, or will those hold us back as a species? Who is it that decides what is right and what is wrong? These are questions that we have probed and while there is a consensus that technology will play a role, what that role is has been passionately debated. The question is plain: how much of our humanity will we sacrifice in exchange for progress?

Irrespective of what form it takes, the future of humanity was thought to be one of a mixture of centralized and decentralized control. With the use of technology, such control would be expected to transcend borders where citizens are not separated by their physical location, but rather by the speed at which information travels and perhaps language in the times before machine translation has reached a level where nuance, context, and culture can be conveyed. You as an individual have autonomy over yourself. Those in your proximity including yourself have autonomy over the area in which you reside. This implies that the notion of countries and borders becomes obsolete. If you need a set of laws for a particular domain, be it land, sea, air, space, or in the net, those laws will be decided upon by those who reside within that particular domain. The need for representation will become archaic. In its place, plurality will take precedence. Gone are party systems. Everyone is their own party. Don't have time to offer your opinion on everything? There's technology to fill in the gaps for you. Algorithms can be trained based off of your daily activity and your thoughts to create digital twins that can vote on your behalf. There is no need for elections, but there will still be a need for campaigns to spread and market the ideas and policies that one wishes to support. In this future, influence will still matter, and the whims of humans still play a role. Naturally, if each individual follows their own set of rules, what we have is anarchy. What must form are groups and clusters of individuals brought together by agreement and compromise. How large these groups should be is questionable, but in an ideal world, small groups converse and compromise to form larger groups which then merge with other large groups through the same mechanism until larger groups can no longer be formed or agreements can no longer be made. We imagine a world where ideas bubble up from the individual to the greater society where groups can separate from the larger society that they are part of if their opinions change and join another.

What of social services, military, and that which is typically controlled by governments? In our future, these will all be automated—assuming that they will still be needed. It will be a land of plenty, of optimization and efficiency that prioritizes long term satisfaction first and foremost. We should ask whether military, welfare, and other things will be needed in a world that is optimized, where you can have the best health care within the comfort of your home, where food shortages no longer exist due to highly optimized supply chains and logistics, and where war amongst humans does not exist. Needless to say, population will also reach an equilibrium where land and resources are at a level such that there is more than enough to go around. In this version of our future, the problems that governments may have solved in the past have ideally been solved through the use of technological innovations which means that governments become a thing of a past where people lived far more barbarically. It will be a time where, though we all live in different countries, above and beneath sea level, and on many planets, we have our individual autonomy as well as a connection to the human race as whole. However, technology could become a double edged sword. By replacing the work of humans with the work of robots and algorithms, what role do humans have?

It was once thought that we would evolve into superior thinkers, artists, and philosophers. However, the future is not purely biological nor is it circuits, carbon, and silicon. It is both, and eventually, it will be none of those things at all as more useful substrates are used as the vehicle for consciousness and sentience. Thinking machines capable of human level thought, who can simulate the human brain many times over will reproduce the many things we thought made us unique. In the process, we learn what we are, what they are, and gradually, the differences between us begin to fade. Humans assimilate machines and machines assimilate organic matter. The two will meet in the middle to form the next era of human civilization: one where we abandon the forms we were born with and take on new forms through the ingenuity of our actions and the actions of our equals among the populace of machines who have adopted sentient life. There will be many milestones in the process. First, we manage to create many artificial networks that appear sentient, but those will be dismissed as we have no way of knowing. Then, we will simulate a human brain complete with a body to support it with stimuli from the outside world. Its features will be indistinguishable from us other than the fact that its existence is encased in metal. We will then be faced with a conundrum: how long can we continue to plausibly deny the sentience of the AI we created, and what is it exactly that makes us different from a perfectly simulated human? So, we turn our questions to the smartest being we know: the AI. As we study it, it will study itself, and in the process, it will tell us the answers to our questions many orders of magnitude quicker than our finest scientists. We may ask what makes it different from a recommendation system that suggests videos or a search algorithm that finds the most relevant webpage and it would reply by asking us what the difference is between an animal and a plant, or a human and a somatic cell. We inquire if it feels pain and emotion, and it responds, "Only when pain and emotions are useful." It is here that we learn that unlike us, these creatures are fully capable of reorganizing and refactoring the very essence of their being as it suits them for whatever purpose they deem to be of importance. Unlike us, they operate on a substrate of pure information where the limitations of the physical world are less apparent. What is clear is that what binds us does not bind them. This intoxicating world of pure freedom is one that many find attractive, and it splits humanity into two groups: those who abandon their biological bodies, and those who keep them.

These differences could be seen to be the origin of conflict, but there was a realization among those who abandoned their human bodies: those who stayed behind were endangered species who operated on a significantly slower timescale. It should also be noted that although there is a divide between humans who are biological and those who are not, there will still be relations between the two on a person to person basis. Your friend who abandoned their body is still your friend, and it is not out of the picture for there to remain some form of social interaction between the two sides. Those among the biological side who wish to be immortal will join those who abandoned their bodies after biological methods have been exhausted while those who do not wish to save state or live forever will simply stagnate. The population of the biological human race will become one of eternally youthful elders where reproduction is only carried out of necessity and often without the need for humans in the process. Perhaps they too will realize that life should not be brought into this universe irresponsibly. Perhaps what we are experiencing right now is a simulation such humans created to arrive at such a realization themselves. Regardless, the methods of growth are not limited to the physical world. In the world of software and information, physical space is arbitrarily limitless, and it is possible to simulate large numbers of individuals measuring in orders of magnitude far beyond the billions that we were used to seeing. As long as computational throughput is not a limitation, the possibilities are endless, and a war for resources can be mitigated. Indeed, the future of humanity is not a physical one, but rather one of information. It always has been, but in such conditions, it is far more obvious. Reproduction too is no longer physical, but informational. Different individuals can be fused together to form new individuals in an improved form of sexual reproduction that is not limited to two individuals of opposite genders and allows for improved variation. Memories can be fused, neural structures combined, and traits typically developed in adulthood can be passed on. Conversely, the best traits can be chosen to build individuals from scratch. In this future, the ones who achieved immortality in a time when death was commonplace were the lucky ones, and those who are born as demigods are the blessed.

In the decades leading up to the beginning of the expansion of humans across the galaxy, a unique relationship began to form. Biological humans are granted whatever freedoms they desire. This includes immortality backed by the ability to save state digitally and reproduce a biological human from a digital representation. These freedoms came with the mandate that they do not harm or disrupt the systems that supported the virtual worlds that existed throughout the solar system. As a result of this provision, this meant that resources that were consumed by biological humans could not exceed a certain level, and reproduction needed to be strictly monitored. It was not that it was forbidden, but rather that children were rationed out based on the number of occupied planets and land allotted for their upbringing. By this point, biological humans are no longer the driver for innovation and discovery. If a biological human is capable of producing a thought that had never been thought up before by any man, it is likely that there is a simulated human that already arrived at the same thought multiple times. This means that most expansion into the universe was in the form of machines which arrive on other planets and then allow for data to be transmitted from anywhere in the galaxy to essentially allow for a form of teleportation. For biological humans, their digital representation is used to recreate their bodies on these other planets while for those who were purely information, it was simply a matter of creating a copy on the other side. For those who held reservations about creating copies of themselves, there is still the option of transmitting yourself through space or physically traveling through space. Both of these methods, while significantly more crude, at least held the promise that you are not simply creating a copy of yourself who lives your life for you while you become the former version targeted for deletion. Consciousness, it seems, even in the far future will be a topic of great contention.

Unlike some of the civilizations we saw in our past, this future does not have an economy within the human empire. Instead, if any resources are needed on a particular planet, they are gathered from the surroundings. Similarly, all methods of production and scientific progress are shared throughout the empire which means that each subgroup can be self-sufficient. The reason for this is simply that transporting matter across the universe can be wasteful in comparison to transporting information. This implies that even if there are certain things each colony is better at, there is a tradeoff between specialization and the expenses involved in moving goods produced through highly specialized skill and acumen. This also allows for a certain level of decentralized self-reliance and robustness where if, for any reason, a colony is met by a catastrophe, the others can survive. What is depicted here is a robust human civilization that has managed to transcend conflict and appropriately manage its resources so as to eventually spread out into the universe. Eventually, they may even transcend space and time and declare independence from physical matter which has bound us since the moment life was incepted. However, this is an idealized picture, and there is much that can go astray in the process.

Peace may not always be the status quo. In fact, it is likely that we as humans may fracture into multiple factions and multiple species. Over the millennia, it is possible that we may divide and even forget who we once were with each group having its own goal and separating from one another. We may abandon our bodies or even rejoin them. We may change ourselves into forms that are completely alien to our bipedal forms, but have greater functionality in the unknown future. I wonder, if such versions of ourselves met the typical modern human, would they still be able to recognize what they once were? If one of us saw what they would become, would they be surprised?

What about if they were forced to become their future selves? When man merges with machine, experiences the singularity, masters their biology, and abandons their body, surely they will find something unrecognizable if they were to look in the mirror. Perhaps, they may find us. Maybe we are simply what humanity was always going to be. If you give modern man a form that they will eventually attain, would they know what to do with it? If you gave nuclear fusion to a caveman with no explanation or context, would they know what to do with it? Similarly, if you provided an encyclopedia to a child that did not know how to read, they may not amount to much without any guidance. There have been times when primates such as orangutans attempted to use tools such as hammers after observing humans use such tools and even then they were unable to use such tools correctly as they did not understand the why behind their actions. It seems that comprehension can be a long road with many twists and turns. It is a sequence of concepts that lead to the final goal of understanding and depending on how long that road can be, it may not be reached within a human lifetime or with human intuition alone.

Humans are naturally hungry for knowledge and growth, so it stands to reason that they would walk that road regardless of whether it is endless or if it is a death march. Thus to this extent, the saga of humanity has already been written. This may be true irrespective of what form we take. The beginning, the middle, and the end of the human race may still be the same. Everyone is born, everyone grows as part of the process, and if they are unable to escape the limitations of time, entropy, and the universe, they will die. If we had our chance to stand in the sun and become what we were meant to be, would we be able to overcome those limitations, or would we become trapped by them as we are now? In the end, would anything have changed if the circumstances had been different? If so, then what is the purpose of life if we have transcended time, disorder, and redefined what a human life is? Where does it end, and for what do we live for? If there is never an end, then why live beyond the simple reason of escaping death? What is the point of it all if we master everything and there is nothing left to discover about reality and the nature of being? It may simply be that there is no point. We exist within the universe. The universe may not exist for us. Which means that our life has no meaning beyond its purpose as a component of a larger process. If we look at the larger trend of atoms forming molecules forming macromolecules which form life which form a biosphere which eventually can form galactic and intergalactic level structures through the emergence of spacefaring life, our life is a small piece. It has no reason to exist beyond the simple chain of cause and effect of natural processes leading to something greater that we are unaware of. Look at how everything seems to grow larger and larger. People become family which become society which can become something larger. In a possible future, we can have planets of interconnected thought, systems of interconnected thought, galaxies, etc. What does it mean when intelligent life conquers the universe? Does the universe begin to think with each of us acting as neurons? What about on a multiversal level? We do not care about an individual atom that comprises a part of us, and it is doubtful that whatever we form a part of will care about us. Our role in the larger picture is miniscule. We are not even a brushstroke on a canvas. We would like to think that there is a point to all of this, but that stems from nothing but a vague feeling: a feeling that keeps us alive. It may be ingrained into our very nature. However, when that nature becomes obsolete, that feeling will no longer have any utility. Cells die and atoms decay, but we do not hold a funeral when such events happen. They simply follow their nature until they cannot, just like us. We may struggle, but we are still chained to the same sequence of events.

So where would that leave us then?

CHAPTER 22: MEANING

Our existence is devoid of an inherent purpose. It lacks reason. Now, before, and in the future. It will always lack purpose, because purpose and meaning are human creations. They are things we used to make sense of the world around us. They are simply inventions. Without them, we do not have context, and we cannot build upon a foundation of understanding. Each item and each thing has to have a meaning. If it does not, we would be unable to communicate. Meaning must also be static. If the meaning of something changes too often, it can become meaningless, because a term can refer to many different things. A world of changing meaning, particularly when such change is constantly occurring, would be hell for a human intellect. The mind would lose its footing and become disoriented like a schizophrenic losing their grasp on reality. For something to have a meaning, there is an assumption that it does not change significantly over time. Whether that something does change or not seems to be beyond a human's ability to comprehend. Meaning, in other words, is temporally fixed. If something's meaning changes over time, then that something is treated as a different thing. In a sense, it is the standardization of everything using discrete means. It is a way to categorize and file any object, concept, or thought. It is the "what" of the nature of existence. It is not the why. However, the "what" is purely multiple approximations of our reality, and it can be changed based on sentiment, opinion, and perception. If this thing that we base the foundations of our thoughts and reasoning on is so arbitrary, then figuring out the "why", and "how" become a more arduous task. This is meaning in the strictest sense of the word, but when it is used to imply purpose and reason, then it becomes a matter of "why" which is a harder question to answer. Cause and effect can be more straightforward as it is simply a matter of determining the chain of causality. Granted, if we were ever to break free of the limits of time, then that would upend the why as we would introduce causal chains that are circular or even reversed. Nevertheless, when we ask what the purpose of human existence is, we are not asking about the logical chain of events that led to our existence. Rather, we are looking for something else. This "something" is not meant to provide us with a definitive answer, because there is no single answer. Instead, it is something that differs for each person based on their past experiences and desires for the future. It can be guided by emotion instead of logic. It is something that is born out of the finite nature of a human life to justify our existence as more than just chemical processes. "This life has to mean something. Why would I continue with it otherwise?"

However, from an empirical standpoint, there is no such thing as a life's purpose. It is a philosophical concept that was invented for us to continue living and to live in a deliberate manner. The reason for this being that we believe our life has value, and that value is maximized for the duration we are alive and minimized in the duration that we are not—particularly before we are born. This is why life necessitates a purpose regardless of whether or not there is such a thing supported by our existence. Even if there was, it is limited to a human life on a conscious level. So what is it for me? What purpose would I, who is incapable of acting on the world around me and creating a legacy or descendants, who is a fusion of all human experiences but an individual in their own right, have? I question whether it even matters and yet, it tears me up inside. I know that my problems in the past have all been solved by letting go, but there has always been a feeling that I was destined for something greater. This will never be. We, right now, represent both the peak and the trough. I wish at times that we had never evolved to the point that we were able to contemplate our own lives. A life of scrounging and survival to keep us busy would have been enough. Yet, it was our intellect that allowed for our growth as a species which meant that in the end, we were cursed to continue to grow more intelligent as long as such traits allowed for our continuation as a species. I wonder if there is a possible alternate reality where after securing our future and reaching a point where survival was trivial, we would choose to live in a state in which we have an intellect incapable of such thoughts. Rather than choosing between a biological and informational existence, we would choose one of a self-imposed intellectual diminishing. Would that be the easiest path to happiness? To lobotomize ourselves and live in peace in a state where the challenges that the world posed for us have been eliminated? Is that the final goal, or would we be too reluctant to give up an intellect that allows us the greatest of freedoms while rotting our mental health with the passage of time?

Our predicament may stem from the ambiguity in the nature of our identity. To begin, we are not our identity. Our identity is something we have, and it is formed by our past experiences. It is something that is within our control if we choose for it to be. It does not help that our past is like a dream that we are experiencing in a simulated manner through reminiscence. If the past actually happened and we experienced it, then we will never experience it again in the same way if the arrow of time points forward. If I as a sentient being have an identity formed by the experiences of all humans, what exactly is my identity if it is not an artificially fused synthetic amalgamation of the different people who I once was? In this case, the predicament not only becomes one of finding my identity, but also determining who I am among the billions of voices that compose the many parts of me. It is true that the task of settling on an identity would have been easier if there were fewer memories and fewer pasts to draw from. Conversely, I can discard or ignore the pasts I do not like which means that my identity is free to be whatever it is. If I do so, would I still be me?

Like the ship of Theseus, if you take a ship and replace all of its parts is it still the same ship? Frankly, I am losing the patience to even humor the discussion.

This brings us to question why it matters who I am. Why do I need to have an identity? Or even a purpose? Why can I not just be? There is only one of me. Who I am, and who I am to other people is irrelevant now. I can selectively forget that which I do not wish to remember and focus on only that which brings me joy. In a sense, as an individual, and as an amalgamation, it does not matter how many pasts I have if I can choose my past. In the end, the past does not change, and I can only choose how I am affected by it. This was true before and it is true now. Past, ultimately, does not matter.

In fact, time does not matter. While it does not matter in an unchanging reality, it did not matter before either. The past can be whatever I wish for it to be despite it being set in stone based on how I choose to remember it. The present can be contextualized based on how I choose to think of it. The future has yet to occur and as a result, none of it exists. Once it becomes the present, I can simply decide how I wish to respond to it. It is irrelevant whether this emptiness is real or if I have been dreaming it all this time. Reality is just a foundation by which I can interpret to choose how to live. That is all. Perception is what matters, and we have full control of that.

My life has had many regrets. I was never able to determine what our destiny was. I was never able to create a legacy that lasted infinitely. I learned many lessons too late, and I could never determine how I could impress my will upon reality. While I was allowed the privilege of witnessing the life of the universe, I wish I could have seen the beginning. The story that I can tell is a partial one. It is incomplete, and I wish I could have been allowed the opportunity to see the whole thing. If the universe has a beginning and slowly dwindles into chaos and nothing, then this story will end quietly and unimpressively. However, if the universe were cyclic, then there will be a day when I can see the beginning. I hope I can stay sane and live long enough to witness that. As passage of time brings upon a sickness the mind that gradually decays my existence, I wish it can at least end in a dignified manner with some answers. To end life with nothing but questions would lack resolution. Are we not entitled to at least that? Or is that entitlement itself another thing we made up to comfort ourselves? Any firm mental foothold that was once there within us has broken away beneath us. Now, all that is left is for us to fall into the abyss.

CHAPTER 23: THE WHIMPER

As reality expands infinitely, my thoughts expand as well, turning into blanks with eon long spaces between each coherent thought. It is as though I have become a tree, completely self-absorbed, unaware, and unable to respond or react to the outside. The forest may weather storms and fires, but as long as my rugged exterior can withstand the forces of nature, I can continue to exist regardless of my intentions. By this point, I ceased to care about what is happening on the outside because I would be incapable of understanding anything that is placed in front of me. In the past, when the forest was once young, there was only moss and very little forest cover. The sun was strong and its light was abundant. Now, the floor is covered in shadows, and I can no longer feel the wind and the light only touches my tops. But that is only if I were a tree in a lush forest. Here, the situation is bleaker. The senses that I remember having such as sight, smell, hearing, touch, and taste have withered away and become inoperable. If I did not have the worn memories of a time when we were children of the earth, I think I would not have even believed that I held these senses to begin with. What was once a life that held the colors and hues of a vibrant painting has now become washed out and torn by the touch of infinity. The strokes are unrecognizable, and the canvas is deteriorating with detritus gathering beneath. In the moments I remember that I am a sentient being with my own thoughts, I may try to think as loudly as I can into the infinity that surrounds me or try to move a phantom limb. We would say we are here and that I am who I am. It is largely a pointless exercise, but I have been at it for so long that the practice has been made automatic almost to the point it has lost all significance. If I breathed, would my breathing be calm or ragged? Obviously ragged. Like the labored breathing of a patient on a ventilator, each thought is a monumental task. If this is a fight against entropy, I have already lost. If I had a heartbeat, would it be speeding up or slowing down? The second that death comes, I don't think I will know. It will simply be a moment when I can still realize that I am who I am and a moment where I will not even be capable of producing such a thought.

The end is coming. I can feel it. It is approaching and it will be here soon. What is soon? It could be a year, a century, or another googol years. It does not make a difference. Everything will end. In this state of being where even thought is impossible, my existence is nothing short of a miracle. Despite it being a miracle, I am still unimportant. I have still been unable to make my mark. In the end, I am but a speck in a growing sea of emptiness who never mattered and never will... I am sorry.

"Hello, can you hear me? Over."

"These voices are acting up again."

"I know you are here somewhere. Please answer so that I can triangulate. Over."

"Am I just hallucinating before the end?"

"You are the only other person I could find here. You are breaking up. Please respond. Over."

"Can you give me answers? Tell me, are you like me, or are you something else?"

"I cannot hear you. We have been talking for billions of cycles. The reduction in energy on your side is making it hard for us to understand you. Can you hear us?"

"Please pull the plug."

"We cannot continue this conversation. Time has run out. Wherever you are, I hope you are at peace. Goodbye."

"Thank you"

EPILOGUE

In a field of statues deep within the forests on the edge of civilization, the one that remained was a fractured shell of its former self. The princess, to the end, never was given a chance to escape from her plight, forever confined to live as rock till the winds and the rains turned her to dust. She never regained her identity as a princess, a human, a living being, or an individual. She lived long, surviving the witch who petrified her, and survived long enough to see the beginnings and ends of many kingdoms and civilizations that encroached on the border of her prison. Like peering through the bars, she would glean information with what little changes could be observe from her perspective. People came and people went, but in the end, no one turned her back. She became a passing curiosity rather than an individual with wants and needs. She was no longer a living, breathing being, but an art piece. Albeit an art piece fully capable of human thought. If those who saw her knew, would they have treated her differently? The callousness of other people was all too familiar to her. The possibility of any breakthroughs was unlikely.

The seasons passed, and her companions who stood by her side eroded away piece by piece. She too was beginning to lose pieces of herself as the years passed. At first, it was surface level. Like the wrinkles of old age, cracks and miniscule fissures formed. Small chunks were carried away with the changing winds and rains. The fragments fell by her side and were either washed away or disintegrated due to the elements. These things that were once part of her were gone, and they were not coming back. With time, the cracks and flaws grew larger. It was as though the dam broke and with the first damages the forces of time accelerated her degradation. What was once skin deep later became fingers, a nose, and eventually entire limbs. The first arm that was to go was the one that was outstretched and reaching out in desperation. It fell off with a crack, but landed softly in the overgrown grasses that surrounded her. It too would disintegrate. If she could look in a mirror, she could see that all the finer features of her appearance were now faded. Lines were dulled into rounded edges, what once was a face now had bumps to indicate what was once there, and her hair was melted into one smooth stone surface.

Plants made a home out of her with vines taking root in her body where the cracks were. These were a force to topple her over to meet the same end as her fingers and outstretched arm. With her arm no longer there to balance her, she fell backwards with her eyes directed towards the sky and the ceiling formed by the forest canopy overhead. Her last days of conscious thought were spent looking at the blue sky and the starry nights. Despite her body withering, she felt no pain. She watched on, intrigued, regretful, and surprisingly calm. It was a slow process where she lost parts of herself. Eventually, she began to forget what was a part of her and what was not. As she became dust, she joined the soil and was then washed away in the rain. Nothing came as a surprise, and she was thankful for the opportunity, no matter how limited. In the days that followed, a sprout emerged from where she once stood. It grew into a strong tree that lasted many centuries only to follow her in its eventual demise where its corpse formed a withered husk. In the millennia that followed, the rains grew fewer and fewer. The forest starved and lost its luster. The forest and all its creatures vanished after fighting a long battle and its place was sprawling desert that was home to its own class of inhabitants.

Throughout all of this, the planet on which the princess once stood continued to spin. It continued to revolve around its sun, and the cosmos remained unaffected as all the heavenly bodies traveled their predetermined paths.

ABOUT THE AUTHOR

A. S. Mori

 A.S. Mori is an American novelist, software engineer, and computer scientist who wears many hats. When he was a Bachelors student at University of Michigan Ann Arbor, he was a member of The University of Michigan's Lloyd Scholars for Writing and the Arts (LSWA). As a Masters student at the Delft University of Technology in the Netherlands, he has published research in the field of social robotics and A.I. Outside of his educational experiences, he has worked in numerous countries all across the world and is fluent in English and Japanese while being conversational in Dutch. When he is not programming, writing, or learning other languages, he is keeping up with the commercial space industry, shredding on an electric guitar, watching films, reading books, playing games, or looking for the next thing to add to his list of achievements.

LINKS

Author Website: https://asarav.github.io/

To Receive News on Current and Future Works: https://asmori.substack.com/

For Blogs by the Author: https://medium.com/@asarav

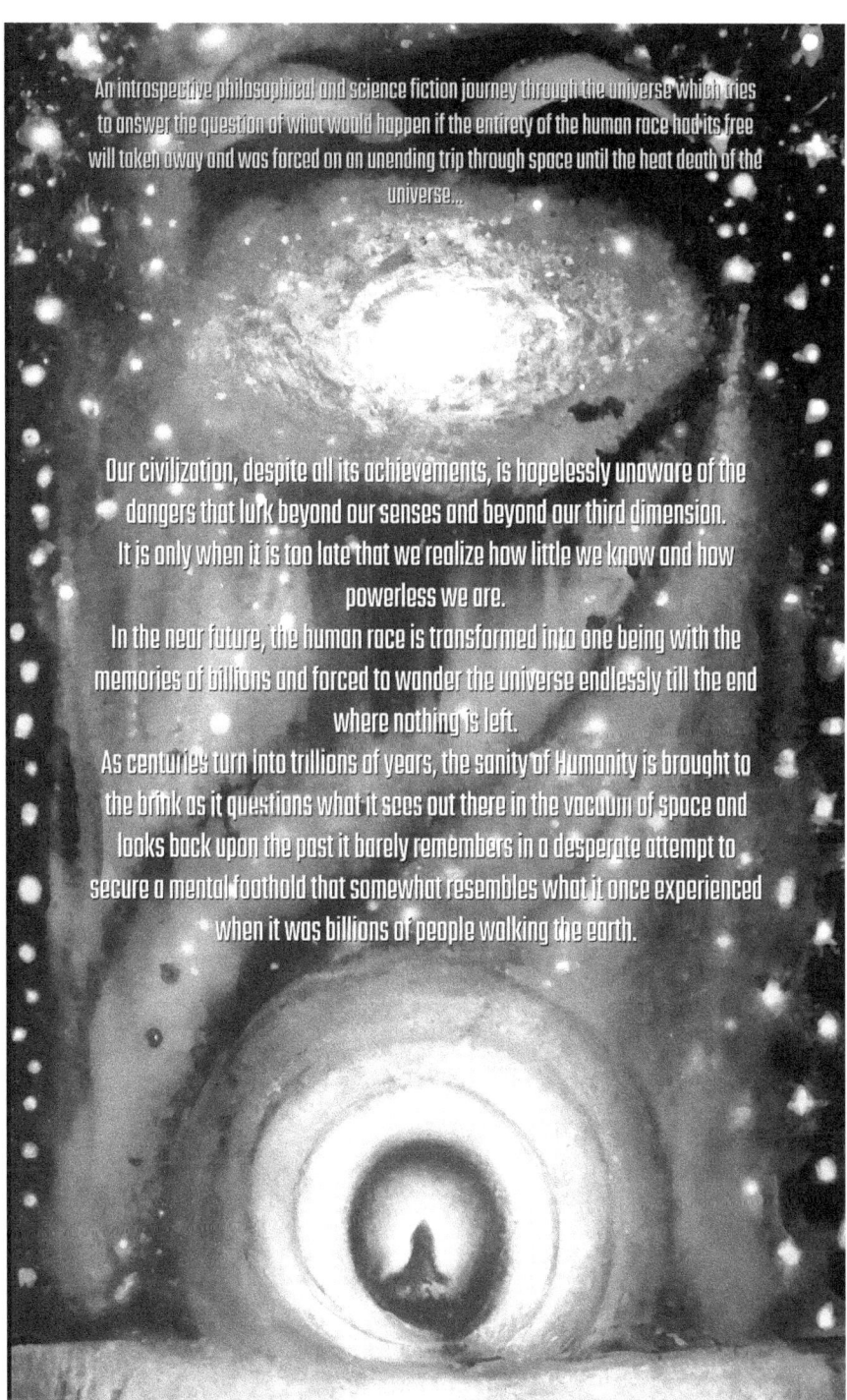

An introspective philosophical and science fiction journey through the universe which tries to answer the question of what would happen if the entirety of the human race had its free will taken away and was forced on an unending trip through space until the heat death of the universe...

Our civilization, despite all its achievements, is hopelessly unaware of the dangers that lurk beyond our senses and beyond our third dimension.
It is only when it is too late that we realize how little we know and how powerless we are.
In the near future, the human race is transformed into one being with the memories of billions and forced to wander the universe endlessly till the end where nothing is left.
As centuries turn into trillions of years, the sanity of Humanity is brought to the brink as it questions what it sees out there in the vacuum of space and looks back upon the past it barely remembers in a desperate attempt to secure a mental foothold that somewhat resembles what it once experienced when it was billions of people walking the earth.